THE

CLASSIC CRIME

LIBRARY

#17

B

STRANGE EMBRACE

Lawrence Block

writing as 'Ben Christopher'

A LAWRENCE BLOCK PRODUCTION

The Classic Crime Library

1. *After the First Death*
2. *Deadly Honeymoon*
3. *Grifter's Game**
4. *The Girl with the Long Green Heart**
5. *The Specialists*
6. *The Triumph of Evil*
7. *Such Men Are Dangerous*
8. *Not Comin' Home to You*
9. *Lucky at Cards**
10. *Killing Castro**
11. *A Diet of Treacle**
12. *You Could Call It Murder*
13. *Coward's Kiss*
14. *Cinderella Sims*
15. *Passport to Peril*
16. *Ariel*
17. *Strange Embrace*
18. *Candy*
19. *Four Lives at the Crossroads*

*Available in paperback from Hard Case Crime

Chapter One

Johnny Lane stood at a window and stared out over Central Park. He was a tall man with an athlete's build and a strong chin. Usually his gray eyes were keen, penetrating. But now they held a vacant expression as he viewed the dark expanse that lay beyond the bright lights of Fifth Avenue.

Central Park, he thought. Muggings, stabbings and rapes. Come and bring the kiddies and we'll all have fun.

He turned decisively from the window and walked with quick firm steps to a heavy Victorian wing chair beside a telephone. He sat down, hoisted the receiver to his ear, dialed a number. He listened impatiently to seven full rings, then slammed down the phone and slumped unhappily in the chair.

He heard the sound of a man clearing his throat.

Johnny turned his head. Ito was standing at his side, holding a small mahogany tray with a tumbler perched in its center. The slender man's face was impassive but his eyes twinkled merrily.

"Master appears troubled," Ito said. "This servant has prepared special potion of esteemed medicinal value. Potion especially useful when user is troubled."

Johnny Lane grinned in spite of himself. "Cut the honorable-son routine," he said. "Save it for company. But thanks for the therapy—it's just what the doctor ordered." He picked up the tumbler and sipped the straight bourbon it contained.

"The girl doesn't answer?"

Johnny shook his head. "The girl doesn't answer. The girl is supposed to be ready for two weeks of out-of-town rehearsals starting tomorrow, and it's a quarter to two in the goddamn morning, and the girl doesn't answer. Where in the name of hell the girl is, I do not know. Who in the name of Sarah Bernhardt the girl thinks she is . . ."

He broke off, shrugged angrily and drank more bourbon. Ito disappeared long enough to get rid of the tray, then returned. The perfect servant, Johnny thought. And every producer needed a perfect servant, just as every producer needed a well-stocked liquor cabinet. Both were essential safeguards against insanity.

He thought that over, tried to decide whether it was original on his part or a line from some play, and decided that it really didn't matter. What mattered was the rest of the bourbon in the glass. He finished it off. He dialed the girl's number again, listened to the phone ring its brains out, and replaced the receiver.

"Damn it," he said. "Now what in hell is the matter with that girl? Ito, it doesn't add up at all. This is the first real part Elaine James has even been within yards of. She's had a few small supporting roles off-Broadway but nothing worth a damn. Now she's set up for the lead in *A Touch of*

Squalor with Ernie Buell directing and Carter Tracy for a co-star. The play is a honey and the part couldn't be better. And with all of seven hours before it's time to grab a train to the hinterlands where is she?"

"I give up," Ito said. "Where is she?"

"Who the hell knows?" Johnny stood up, walked once more to the window. "Maybe she's over there, Ito. Maybe she's necking shamelessly on a park bench. Maybe she's in some guy's bed having a going-away party."

"Is honorable master jealous?"

"Is honorable servant becoming nosy?" Johnny's face relaxed into a grin. "You should know me better than that, Ito. Business and pleasure can't be combined. Not in this racket, anyhow. A producer who sleeps with his leading lady before the show opens is going to end up with a turkey."

"And after the show opens?"

"She's a lovely girl," Johnny admitted. "Very sweet and very bright." He returned to his chair and sank into it. "And what happens after the show opens," he went on, "is none of your damned business."

Ito recaptured Johnny's empty glass and left the room. Not because he, Ito, was insulted—he had long since proved himself impervious to insult—but because he sensed that Johnny wished to be alone. He was right. Johnny took a cigarette from the pack in his jacket pocket, put it into his mouth and scratched a match. He dragged deeply and filled his lungs. He blew out smoke and again glanced at his watch.

Two o'clock. Two a.m. and Elaine was still out on the town. Well, what the hell was he worrying about? She was a big girl, old enough to decide when to go to bed. And with whom, he thought sullenly. Besides, why was he trying to reach her in the first place? To tell her not to miss the train? That was brilliant. Hell, even if he got her on the phone he wouldn't have a thing to say.

He closed his eyes—which was pleasant, and pictured Elaine James in his mind—which was even more pleasant. Twenty-two years old, five-and-a-half feet tall, with all the requisite curves in their proper places. A red rosebud of a mouth that was designed for gentle kissing. Soft light-blond hair in a Dutch cut, a hairstyle damned few girls could get away with, and in which she looked childishly magnificent. Light blue eyes, cool eyes. An amazingly beautiful girl, all things considered.

But why did he want to assure himself that she was home? He toyed with the idea that it was a purely glandular reaction. But that didn't make any sense. When you were busting your hump trying to get a show on the boards, just two weeks remaining before you were supposed to open in New Haven, you didn't make passes at your leading lady. And Elaine had not struck him as much of a pass receiver anyway; there was something annoyingly virginal about her.

Why, then?

He stood up. "Ito!" he yelled. And he strode to the hall closet, opened the door and grabbed a topcoat.

"I'm going out," he told his butler. "I'm chasing a wild goose."

"The girl?"

"Don't ask why, because I don't know myself. Just a hunch, I guess. Something doesn't seem right. I'm probably nuts but I want to make sure."

A gray-faced, thin-lipped elevator operator piloted Johnny down sixteen flights from the penthouse to the lobby. Johnny was privately convinced that the man, whose name he had never managed to determine, had not spoken since the Spanish-American War. Now the operator maintained his clean record and Johnny matched him word for word. Then Johnny passed through the lobby and went out into the cool crisp air of nighttime New York, crossed Fifth and grabbed a cab headed downtown.

"Six sixty-one East Fifth Street," he told the driver.

"You sure that ain't in the East River, Mac?"

"Almost," Johnny admitted. "Between Avenue B and C. Take the Drive down."

"That's a long way from Fifth and Sixty-first," the cabby said.

Johnny agreed with him silently. It was a long way in more ways than one, he thought. A long way from a penthouse with a park view to a railroad flat on the fifth floor of a building that should have been condemned when Lindbergh crossed the Atlantic. But girls like Elaine James didn't live in penthouses. When you were a trying-to-make-it actress who worked fifteen weeks out of fifty-two you took whatever you could get. Which, nine times out of ten, meant the Lower East Side.

The cab made good time on the East River Drive. They left the drive at the Tenth Street exit, cut through Riis Project, followed Avenue D to Fifth Street and number 661. Johnny paid the cabby, waved him away.

Standing on the curb, looking up at the faded tenement, Johnny wondered how anyone could live in it. From Fifth Avenue to Fifth Street was a trip to another world.

Well, Elaine James wouldn't be living here long, he thought. She had talent and now her break was coming. *A Touch of Squalor* was a hell of a play. It would put her name in lights for a good long time and the lights would be bright ones. She would move out of her cold-water flat the day the critics told the public just how great she was.

Johnny walked to the door, opened it. The vestibule needed sweeping and painting. There were no doorbells, just a row of rusted iron mailboxes with tenants' names scratched on them. He found one marked Elaine James— 5D. He opened the inner door and walked into the building.

Inside the dirt was dirtier. The stairwell reeked of cooking, stale beer and human sweat, an irresistible combination. Penciled obscenities were misspelled on the walls. Johnny climbed four flights of stairs and cursed industriously all the way. He was breathing heavily when he reached the fifth and top floor.

I'll be damned, he thought. She's got the penthouse. And he laughed.

There were four apartments on the floor and he looked at all four doors before he found 5-D. A small card, carefully lettered, announced that Elaine James lived inside. There was no doorbell. He knocked.

No sound came from within. Well, what did you expect? he wondered. You damn fool, if she were home she would have answered the phone.

He tried the door on impulse. The knob stuck, but once he managed to coax it into turning the door swung open, creaking horribly as it did so. He hesitated in the doorway, looking at the darkness and wondering what the hell he was doing here. She was out and the door was open and he should close it and get the hell out himself. But it just was not like Elaine to leave a door unlocked. She was a careful, methodical person.

Which, come to think of it, was the reason it wasn't like Elaine to be out on the town at two-thirty in the morning when she had a nine o'clock train to catch.

And the door was open. Of course in that neighborhood it might mean simply that the lock was defective. Still, he wanted to check. It couldn't hurt.

He fumbled around on both sides of the door looking for a light switch. He gave up and struck a match. A metal chain dangled from a ceiling fixture in the middle of the room. He walked to it, yanked it, and the light went on.

The apartment looked as though it belonged in another building. The room—the living room, he guessed—was furnished inexpensively but well. It was small and at one end there were cooking arrangements—a two-burner hot-plate and an archaic sink—but the room was happily homey. The carpet on the floor was clean, if far from new. And the walls had been painted a pleasant beige.

Johnny closed the door, then surveyed the room again. Elaine's reading matter was stacked neatly on the coffee table. Copies of *Variety* and *Show Business*, a few numbers of the *Village Voice,* a half-dozen paperbacks. He looked through the books, raised his eyebrows at titles like *The Jungian Approach to Dramatic Reality*, *The Cartesian Ethic in the Theatre*, and *Theatrical Gestalt in Twentieth Century America.* He replaced the books gingerly, wondering what in the world their titles meant, then took a cigarette from his pack, struck a match and scorched his throat again with smoke.

There were two doors at the far end of the living room. He walked to one, knocked carefully, and finally eased it open. He saw a small closet, containing an overcoat and a pair of galoshes. He wondered why he had knocked and thought how strange it would have been if the galoshes had answered him. He closed the closet door and knocked loudly on the other door.

The bedroom, he thought. And if nobody answers I should not—repeat not—open the door.

Nobody answered.

So he opened the door.

The bedroom light was on. A soft yellow glow bounced

off the beige walls and the dark carpet. The room was tiny, with space only for a single bed and a chest of drawers. One ancient suitcase stood at the side of the chest of drawers.

The blankets were bunched up at the foot of the bed. A sheet covered the mattress. Elaine James lay on top of the bed on her back. She was nude.

He looked at her. He studied her nakedness shamelessly, because neither he nor she had anything to be ashamed of now. He looked at the perfectly tapered legs, at the firm proud breasts.

His stomach turned over. His cigarette dropped from his fingers to the floor and he ground it into the carpet with his heel.

Elaine James was a lovely girl, she was lovely from the neck down. She was also lovely from the neck up.

But her neck was not lovely at all, because somebody had slashed a hole in it.

There was a telephone on top of the dresser. He used a handkerchief to lift the receiver to his ear. His eyes focused hazily on the dial and he remembered listening to this same telephone ring and ring. And he had cursed the girl for not being there to answer it. She had been there, most likely. But in no condition to answer.

He felt numb. He managed to dial the right number, and he managed to ask the desk sergeant for Lieutenant Haig. Seconds later he heard Haig's voice. It was flat and tired and it fitted Johnny's mood.

"Homicide. Haig speaking."

"Sam, this is Johnny. Johnny Lane."

"Johnny? Hell, I thought you were getting out of town."

"Not until tomorrow," he said. "Well, today, really. Nine o'clock train. Sam, there's . . . there's been a murder. I found a body."

A low whistle came over the phone.

"Six Sixty-one East Fifth Street. That's between B and C. Apartment 5-D. You'd better get over here."

"You there now?"

"I'm here."

"Stay there, then. I'll be right up. Who got it, Johnny? Somebody you know?"

"I knew her. A girl named Elaine James. My—uh—my leading lady. You better hurry, Sam."

He hung up the phone, put his handkerchief back into his pocket and turned around slowly. He saw Elaine again, saw what had been Elaine, and nausea climbed in his throat. Her blood had soaked into the sheet. Some of it had trailed down into the valley between her breasts.

He walked out, closed the door. He sat down on the couch in the living room and waited. He picked up a recent issue of *Variety* and tried to kill a few minutes reading it but the print danced before his eyes. All he could see was Elaine, so nude and so dead, lying in a room where a phone rang again and again.

Theatrical, he thought. A good dramatic touch. Maybe a little too vivid, but loaded with impact.

Haig was on his way. Haig was sharp and thorough, and he would get hold of the bastard who slashed her.

Johnny hoped they caught him fast and killed him dead as hell.

Chapter Two

"She must have been pretty," Haig said. "Once, I bet, she must have been pretty."

"She was," Johnny said.

They were in the bedroom. Haig's lab men were being busy, measuring distances, dusting for fingerprints, picking up dirt samples and doing other mysteriously scientific things which Johnny did not pretend to understand. He stood with Haig at the side of the bed. Now a thin white sheet covered Elaine James' body, stopping an inch or two below the gash across her throat.

Haig cleared his throat. He was a big man, heavy, with gray mixed into his black hair. He was not a pretty man. His nose had been broken twice and he had scar tissue around the eyes. He was a good cop and he and Johnny had been friends for years.

"Some people would say she's still pretty," Haig went on. "Maybe she is. I don't know. Once they're dead they stop looking good to me. All I can see is the death part of it. The ugliness. There's nothing pretty about death."

Johnny assented silently.

"I oughta get used to it," Haig said. "I see enough of

them. Cuttings, stabbings, shootings—the works. You know what we had a week ago? A garroting. Got any idea what a garroting looks like?"

"A fair idea."

Haig shrugged. "We found this guy in the park. Central Park. Damn fool was walking through Central Park at three in the morning. You got to be a real clown to walk through Central Park at that hour. Pretty when we found him. His head swelled up and turned purple. A purple basketball with the eyes three-quarters out of their sockets. Pretty."

"No worse than this," Johnny said. "It couldn't have been worse than this."

"Who knows? To me they're all the same and I never get used to them. Maybe I'm in the wrong business." He sighed heavily. "We might as well get out of here. The microscope boys can do more than we can. We only get in their way. Amazing guys. They can take the lint from a man's pants cuffs and tell you who he's been sleeping with. They'll turn up something."

"They'll turn up a few thousand fingerprints that belong to me," Johnny said. "I must have handled half the apartment. I didn't know I was going to find a corpse." His eyes returned to the wound on the girl's neck. "You know what killed her?"

"Something sharp, most likely."

"Thanks a lot."

"Hell," Sam Haig said. "Who knows? Maybe a big knife, a long one. Maybe a razor. The lab boys will study it and find out it's a Malayan kris stolen from the British Museum in eighteen-fourteen. They're amazing."

"If they're so good, why do they keep you on the force?"

The big cop grinned. "They need a rough son-of-a-bitch to beat up suspects. And to crash through doors with a gun in his fist. Like in the movies. Let's get out of here, huh? I have to keep you up all night answering questions. You might miss your train."

Ito answered the phone almost at once. "Honorable Mister Lane's residence," he intoned. "Humble servant speaking."

"Can it," Johnny said "It's only me."

"I was wondering where you were."

"I'm in Haig's office, Ito. Somebody found Elaine James before I did. Somebody slit her throat." He stopped to catch his breath. "Ito, there's a list of people connected with the show in the top drawer of my desk. Call everybody on the list, tell them to miss the train and wait for further instructions. We'll be delayed a few days at least, maybe more."

"Do I tell them why?"

"No. Just that I said so. They'll find out soon enough anyway, but in the meantime they might as well stay in the dark. Call them and tell them no train, period. And don't wait up for me. I'll be a while."

"I'll be up," Ito said.

"Don't you ever sleep?"

"Only in the winter," Ito said.

Johnny laughed and hung up, then looked across the

desk at Haig. "That's out of the way," he said. "Now you're supposed to ask me probing questions."

Haig nodded sleepily. "You kill her, Johnny?"

"What!"

"Well, I had to ask. It says so in the book. Any idea who did it?"

"None."

"It wasn't robbery," Haig said. "She had a pearl ring on one finger and we found a few bucks in plain sight in a dresser drawer."

"Is it still there?"

"Naturally. Cops only rob the living. Anyway, it wasn't a burglar. Nothing ransacked. So it was sex or some personal-type motive."

Johnny nodded. "I can't think of anybody who would have any reason to kill her," he said. "Not offhand."

"Know much about her?"

"Not too much."

"Let's have what you know."

Johnny lit a cigarette. "Her name's Elaine James," he said. "It is now, anyway. She may have changed it somewhere along the line. She's been in New York for two, three years looking for a break. The usual routine—temporary office help to pay the rent, a round of auditions that didn't pan out. An occasional bit off-Broadway but never with a show that caught on. When I held open auditions for *A Touch of Squalor* she stood in line with a few hundred other girls. I took one look at her and saw that she'd be perfect for the lead if she could act worth a damn. So she read for it and she was perfect. A hell of a fine actress."

"So she could act. That all you know about her?"

"Almost all," Johnny admitted. "She came from a little town upstate. She was too young to have graduated from college and still spend two or three years in New York and die at twenty-two. Maybe she went to a junior college, I don't know."

"We'll find out."

"That's the point—I don't think there's much I can tell you that you couldn't turn up anyway. She lived alone. She was friendly enough with everybody in the show but none of them were close friends by any means. She hadn't known them long enough for that."

"Was she sleeping with anybody?"

"Not that I know of. I had a feeling she might be a virgin."

"Any reason to think so?"

"Just a hunch."

"I didn't think there were any virgins left in the world," Haig said. "Well, we'll find that out by morning when the Medical Examiner's report comes in. That and other things. If she was raped. If she was pregnant. Anything like that, we'll find out. You get yourself murdered and you don't have any privacy at all. It's one hell of a thing."

The big cop picked up a letter opener and began to clean his nails with it. "Let's take the rest of the cast," he suggested. "Maybe one of them had it in for her."

Johnny frowned. "That's pretty hard to believe."

"Is it? If you know as much about them as you know about the James girl, they could all be orangutans and you wouldn't know the difference. Who's in the show?"

"Carter Tracy is her co-star. Was her co-star. Hell, it's wrong either way. How do you say it when it's like this?"

"Death fouls up tenses," Haig said.

"He's the leading man. That does it. You know who he is?"

"I've seen him in the movies, if that's what you mean. Mostly late movies on television. Isn't he a little old for our girl?"

Johnny nodded. "He's about fifty, I think. Admits to forty-two, which is impossible. See, the age difference was the point of it. The plot of the play spins around an inge- nue type who falls for a smooth old bastard. Tracy plays the bastard and Elaine was supposed to play the sweet young thing."

"Sounds like typecasting. Tracy really is a bastard, isn't he?"

"He's all wrapped up in his own ego," Johnny said. "It amounts to almost the same thing. But he's one hell of a good actor, and good actors are all egotistical. It's an oc- cupational disease. Besides, his ego hasn't been up so high lately. He's slumped. Hollywood doesn't seem to think he's a leading man anymore. He was ready to crawl for this part, figuring that it could make all the difference in the world to him. It's an older part and a romantic role all at once, a handy bridge between two camps."

"Who else?"

Johnny looked at Haig. He was taking brief but careful notes on a legal-sized pad of ruled yellow paper. "I suppose Jan Vernon is next," Johnny said. "Know her?"

"Name rings a bell."

"She hasn't made any movies recently. She was a starlet in Hollywood for a while, then switched to Broadway. She had the lead in *The Levantine Factor* and good supporting roles in *Under Black Skies* and *Last Thursday*."

"What is she? The prim and proper type?"

Johnny laughed. He pictured Jan in his mind, thought of the sleepily voluptuous figure, the pouting mouth, the lay-me look that never left her eyes, not even when she was doing something as prosaic as counting her lines.

"Not exactly," he said. "Not quite prim and proper. In our play she's cast as Elaine's older cousin. The one who's been around until she's a little frayed at the edges. Carter Tracy bangs her while he's making the pitch for Elaine. Get the picture?"

"Uh-huh. Tracy banging her off-stage as well as on?"

"Damned if I know. If he isn't, he can't be trying."

"Another case of typecasting?"

Johnny shrugged. "Who knows? You never know what to believe in this business. Everything is a rumor. She's supposed to have figured in a few choice parties out on the Coast. The orgy set, you know. A little marijuana and a little juice and away we go. There was an arrest, according to this rumor, but she was under contract at the time and her studio managed to put the lid on it. The rumor routine may be so much nonsense, but if she's got more morals than an alley cat then I'm Jack the Ripper."

"That leaves the question open, friend. Keep going."

"Reuben Flood is the lead's father. The name won't even ring a bell, but you'd recognize the face. He's been in a few hundred movies and God knows how many plays. A trouper all the way, one of the best damn character actors in the business. Stan Harris plays the lead's older brother. He's a young kid, just starting out. The part is a small one and he's right for it and that's about all I know about him. Tony Foy has a bit part—he's another young hopeful—and there are maybe five or six walk-ons. That takes care of the cast."

"Understudies?"

"Uh-huh. But don't ask me who they are, because I'd have to look them up to tell you. And don't think that Elaine's understudy killed her to inherit the part. She wouldn't get it. The understudies are just insurance in case one of the cast comes down with a bad hangover or something. They wouldn't serve as permanent replacements."

Johnny drummed his fingers on the desktop, pausing to think things out. The little recitation he'd given was fine for Haig's notebook—it filled up plenty of yellow paper. But it wasn't going to nail any killer to the wall.

Hell, it was just a matter of form. In the morning the Medical Examiner would establish that Elaine had been raped and then murdered and the killing would be designated a pointless sex slaying. That would make fine copy for the tabloids, but it would also mean that there would be no way he could help. If the killer were caught at all, it would be police procedure that did the trick— not one Johnny Lane.

"The director is Ernest Buell," Johnny continued. "A temperamental guy maybe a little bit nuts. He's been in one rest home or another off and on for fifteen years. He isn't a complete nut, though. It's just that he gets depressed. It seems to be an occupational disease. A few weeks away from Broadway and he's all right again."

"What they ought to have," Haig said, "is a rest home for cops. Lieutenants in particular. For days when I get depressed."

Johnny laughed. Then he thought about the girl, Elaine, and about the fiend who had killed her. The laughter died.

"To hell with it," he said. "I could tell you what color cat our assistant stage manager has and who planned the lighting and a million other damn fool things and it wouldn't get us anywhere. What it boils down to is that I don't know anything. Somebody killed her. I wish he hadn't. Period."

"Sure, Johnny. It's a mess. I ask questions because I have to. Then we find out it was a sex killing and we have to start all over again. We throw out a net and catch perverts, and we make all the perverts tell us what they were doing at the time and with whom, and maybe we get the bastard and maybe we don't." He held up his sheet of notes. "This," he said, "I could throw it in the garbage and it wouldn't matter."

"I'll see you," Johnny said. He stood up. "You'll have to solve this one without me, Sam. But let me know when the ME report comes in, right?"

"Of course," Haig told him. "And you keep your crew of hams in town until they're cleared." He smiled sadly. "You won't be able to go into action for a while in any case, will you? Not with your leading lady waiting to be replaced. I guess it's been a bad night all around, huh?"

Johnny agreed with him.

Ito was still up. Johnny got rid of his hat and coat and found a chair to sink into. Then he gave Ito a full summary of the night's activities. The butler's face remained impassive.

"Hell of a thing," Ito said. "If whoever raped her waited one more day she'd have been all right. She'd have been out of town."

"I know. It's quite a coincidence."

"What do you think?"

"I don't know. Somehow I can't swallow the sex-killing bit. I've got a theatrical mind, Ito. I want a plot to dovetail neatly. The police have the right idea. They question everybody until one person looks wrong. They throw questions at half the town until one guy can't answer them straight. And nine times out of ten the first one they pick is guilty." He lit a cigarette. "I want it more complex than that, damn it. She—she died in a strange way. She couldn't have put up much of a fight at all. She looked almost peaceful, for the love of God! As though she'd been sleeping when he . . . cut her throat."

"Does she always sleep nude?"

"How the hell would I know? All right, you can stop laughing at me now. I fell for it. Any calls while I was out?"

Ito told him there were none. Johnny finished his cigarette, then stood up.

"I'm going to sleep," he announced. "I've got a hell of a lot to do tomorrow. I'll have to check out all the girls around who might be candidates for Elaine's part. If I find a fast study in a hurry we may be able to open in time."

"Really?"

"Really," Johnny said. "With only two weeks for the leading lady to learn to tell her lines from her behind, we'll be lousy in New Haven. But we can straighten it out in time for the New York opening. Look, it's six now. Do you think you can be up by noon?"

"I'll be up at ten. Should I wake you at noon?"

"Yeah, wake me at noon," Johnny said. "But how in hell will you manage to be up at ten?"

"You know, we Orientals are wonderfully industrious," Ito said. "And inscrutable. You can never tell what we're thinking—"

"Go get some sleep," Johnny said, then headed out of the room.

Chapter Three

Johnny Lane came out of sleep slowly, groggily. Ito was shaking him, attempting to be both gentle and firm at once. Johnny's eyes opened and the light was painful.

"Go away," he said sourly. "Go join your honorable ancestors or something."

"Mr. Lane—"

Johnny groaned. "God," he said. "It can't be noon yet."

"It isn't."

"What the—"

"It's eleven-thirty, which is close. And you have company. A visitor."

"Haig?"

Ito shook his head. "Not even close," he said. "A woman. An attractive woman. She insists that her name is Jan Vernon and that she has to see you at once."

"What does she look like?"

Ito thought it over. "She looks as though she was slept with not long ago."

"Then it's Jan," Johnny said, grinning. "And she probably was. Tell her to sit down and relax while I try to turn back into a human being. She probably needs some coffee. Me, too. With vitamins in it."

"Vitamin B for bourbon?"

Johnny nodded. He wondered how long it would take him to wake up. Quite a while, he decided.

A shower helped. So did a shave. He brushed his teeth to remove their fur coat and splashed cold water on his face. He dressed in a hurry, putting on a sport shirt and a pair of light flannel slacks. He broke his shoelaces trying to tie them, threw the shoes away and put on a pair of loafers instead.

A hot cup of fortified coffee was waiting for him in the living room. So was Jan Vernon.

"Johnny," she said, "I'm scared."

"I'm exhausted," he told her. He sat down and took a sip of the coffee to clear away mental cobwebs. There was a lonely cigarette in the tray on the coffee table. He lit it and smoked, studying Jan at the same time.

Ito was right, he decided. She definitely looked as though she had been slept with, and recently. The black hair that cascaded over her shoulders managed to look mussed up, even when every strand was in its place. The mouth pouted even when she smiled. And the eyes beckoned provocatively even when she was scared, which she obviously was now.

"I'm scared," she said.

"You heard about Elaine?"

She nodded, her face grim. "Some policeman came banging on my door in the middle of the night."

"Haig?"

"That's the one. He was halfway through the story before I figured out what he was talking about. At that point I started to shake. I'm still shaking."

"It was something to shake about," Johnny told her. "A pretty rugged scene."

"You found the . . . body?"

"Uh-huh. Didn't Haig tell you?"

"He probably did. I was a little out of it at the time. Johnny, are we still going through with the show?"

He nodded. "Sure," he said. "We may get going a week late at the outside, but I doubt it. I'll call around and dig up another lead. I know it sounds ghoulish but that's show biz, to coin a phrase."

"The show must go on?"

"Uh-huh. A lot of backers have a lot of dough in this. Why? You sound like you think we ought to dump the thing, Jan."

The eyes clouded, then turned to the floor. "Maybe we should," she muttered. "Maybe we should."

"Huh?"

She sighed. "I told you I was scared," she said. "I'm not scared because I'm a woman and a vicious killer is walking the streets. That's garbage. I don't scare that easily, Johnny. I've got a better reason than that."

He was interested. "Okay," he said, "let's hear it."

"I'm scared because I'm in *A Touch of Squalor.*"

Johnny stared at her. "You heard me," she went on, "Somebody has it in for this show, Johnny. Somebody who wants to keep us from opening in the worst way. I don't believe this sex-nut story. I don't believe it at all. I think Elaine was murdered because she had the lead in the show."

"You been smoking the wrong kind of cigarettes again, Jan?"

Her temper flared. "That was a damn lie," she snapped. "And if you'd wait a goddamn minute you'd find out what I'm talking about."

"I'm sorry."

"You should be. I've had three phone calls," she said. "Three times a male voice has told me to drop the show cold or get my head handed to me. I was supposed to quit or get killed—that was the message."

"And you didn't tell me about it?"

"I thought it was a gag. An actor making jokes. It's the kind of joke an actor makes, isn't it?"

"I suppose so. Did the—this voice—did it say anything else?"

"Just that somebody important didn't want the show to open. That was all. Johnny, I didn't even think about it the first time. The second time it wasn't funny anymore but it still seemed like a gag. When the third call came I was pretty teed-off. I gave the guy on the other end of the phone a few choice directions and slammed the phone down hard enough to hurt his ear. Then later on I was thinking about it again. I was with Elaine and I mentioned the calls to her. I asked her if she thought they were a gag."

"How did she take it? Did she laugh?"

"Like you laugh at a funeral, that's how she laughed. She went white in the face and her hands started to shake. I told her to relax, it was only a joke, and besides, I was the one he was threatening. And she repeated that of course it was a joke. And she calmed down, or put on a good act."

Johnny nodded. Maybe Jan wasn't out of her head at all. Maybe she had gotten hold of something—something not very pretty.

"Well, Johnny, what do you think?"

"The same as you, probably. She must have received similar calls herself. And when you told her she wasn't the only one..."

"She took it seriously." Jan sighed.

Johnny closed his eyes and tried to think straight. He was damned if he knew who would want to keep a play from opening. There were people who tried to make sure plays closed early—they called themselves critics—but few who didn't want a show to open in the first place. It didn't make any sense.

What if he postponed rehearsals a month and delayed the opening by that much time? The backers would not be able to wriggle free; the money was already committed. The delay would run into a certain amount of money but the play was a strong enough property to carry through.

He frowned. It wouldn't work—he couldn't announce it as a delay or the murderer, whoever he was, would still be out for blood to prevent the show from opening at a later time. And he couldn't fake it through by announcing that the show was cancelling itself or there would be hell to pay. The backers would demand their cash and the cast would look around for other work. Could he call it a closing while cluing in cast and backers to the truth? No, he couldn't, he thought. Because he might manage to clue in the murderer in the process.

"Ito!" he bellowed. The servant came on the run, bowing for Jan's benefit. "Call the cast," he said. "We'll be staying in the city until further notice. I'm busy looking for the right replacement for Elaine James and our opening will probably be postponed two weeks, maybe longer. Everybody should get his lines down pat and do a lot of constructive thinking about his part. Got it?"

Ito nodded.

Johnny paced, trying to think straight. "Better call the trade papers, too. Give them the same news but phrase it differently. We're all broken up over what happened to Elaine and we're taking a two-week break to honor her memory, or something like that. Everybody will figure out what that means but it looks better in print. Otherwise they'll think I'm a cold-hearted bastard."

Ito nodded again and went looking for a telephone. When they were alone Jan looked at Johnny and smiled grimly. "You," she said, "are a cold-hearted bastard."

"I probably am," he agreed. He finished the combination of coffee and bourbon and got another cigarette going. His mind was working much better now and his body was not objecting quite so strenuously to the lack of sleep. His body, as a matter of fact, was proving that it was alive. The presence of Jan Vernon was having a disconcerting effect upon him.

If Jan could project sexiness from the stage to the

balcony—and she definitely could—the effect was greatly increased in the privacy of a living room. She did not seem as frightened now as when she had arrived. She was relaxed in her chair, one leg crossed over the other at the knee, and Johnny had trouble keeping his eyes from her limbs.

They were good limbs and she knew it. There was nothing wrong with the rest of her, either, and she knew this as well. She would not have worn tight sweaters, for example, if she were not thoroughly satisfied with the quality and quantity of her mammary equipment.

The elaborately rumpled hair and the pouting mouth did not detract either. The play of the breasts within the sweater when she yawned and stretched was no soothing balm. Obviously, Jan's position in life was basically a horizontal one and Johnny struggled with a strong urge to haul her off to the bedroom and ravish her. He had a hunch she would not mind at all.

Johnny sighed and switched back to business. "You didn't tell Haig about the phone calls, did you?"

"I didn't think about them. Why?"

"Just an idea," he said. "If he ties it to the show none of us will have time to breathe. I'd rather sound out the rest of the cast first and find out who's been getting the same kind of call, if anyone has. And there's still the chance that this is a fluke—a sex-killing coincidentally tied in with a not-too-practical joke."

She looked at him quizzically. "You don't really believe that, do you?"

"I don't know what I believe. I'll have Ito set up a cast

meeting for this evening. Over here, say, at eight o'clock. Just the principal players, plus Ernie—if some joker is trying to stop the show he won't bother frightening bit players. We can sit around together over a drink or two and get everything out into the open. It'll clear the air. Because if anybody else has been getting phone calls and hasn't mentioned it, he's scared out of his wits."

"I know what you mean," Jan said. "I'm a little steadier now that I told you. Johnny, why don't we have the meeting at my place? It's certainly big enough—I've been rattling around in it since I got rid of my last husband. And it's more convenient. Most of the people in the show live downtown."

"Well..."

"And I'm a sissy," she said, grinning. "The less I go out at night the better I like it."

"Good enough. You're around the corner from Gramercy Park, right?"

"Right."

"Expect company at eight, then. We shouldn't take too long."

"That's fine," she told him. "And if you get there a little early, that's also fine. My coffee is every bit as good as Ito's, you know. And I may think of something I'll want to tell you in private."

He saw her to the door, then paced the living room. The last bit of byplay had been an open enough invitation, especially in view of the fact that Jan Vernon had done the inviting. Which raised an interesting ethical question. It was bad form for the producer to sleep with his leading lady, true. But what about the second lead?

He thought of writing to *Variety* and asking them. He laughed softly, then went to the telephone to get busy calling agents. But he couldn't get the idea completely out of his mind. Whatever the ethics of the situation, he was sure it would be a pleasant experience to share Jan Vernon's bed.

The phone rang harshly. Johnny picked it up in the middle of the first ring and snapped a *hello* into the mouthpiece.

"You're a tough man to get hold of," Haig barked. "You leave your phone off the hook? I've been calling you for the past half hour or so."

"I was fighting with agents. Why?"

"I have the Medical Examiner's report," the Homicide lieutenant said. "And we can probably forget the sex-killing theory. At least, it wasn't rape."

"Nobody touched her?"

"Just with a razor. That's what it was, incidentally. I didn't think anybody used a straight razor anymore. I've had an electric for the past ten years."

"I use a safety razor. I can't get close enough with an electric."

"Now that's very interesting," Haig said sarcastically. "I guess that proves you didn't kill the girl. I'm glad to hear that. You have no idea how glad . . ."

"I—"

"Now do you want to know what we found out or would you like to tell me what soap you use in the shower?"

Johnny did not say anything.

Haig said, "Okay—the ME fixed time of death at twelve or twelve-thirty that night. He says the girl wasn't pregnant, which wasn't too much of a surprise. He also said she was a virgin, which is. That was your guess, wasn't it?"

"Uh-huh."

"The lab turned the place upside down. The girl's prints were all over everything, of course. But there was one other set of prints that turned up on everything that would hold a print. And we identified them."

"Who did they belong to?"

"You," Haig said.

"Oh."

"We're in a fairly blind alley," the cop said. "It could still be sex. The nude body and the razor—they can fit in. Not every pervert is a rapist. Some nut might get his kicks just using his razor."

"But you don't think so?"

Haig's voice was tired. "I don't think so. I think somebody didn't like the girl very much. I think somebody disliked her enough to slit her throat. Now all I have to do is find out who the somebody is. Just routine, ma'am. All we need are the facts."

"What facts have you got so far?"

"I've been bothering your cast. One kid was going out with the James girl on a fairly regular basis. What's-his-name—Stan Harris. The one who plays her older brother."

Johnny grunted. He hadn't known that.

"There's a funny bit in there. He was willing to admit that he was dating her. So we asked him if he was sleeping with her and he blushed a little and said that he was. Which was tricky, since the girl was a virgin. We hit him with that one and he blushed a little more and got his tongue tangled up in his teeth."

"And?"

"We put two and two together," Haig said. "The normal procedure. We figured she wouldn't come across so he killed her. You know what cops are like. Stupid, crude people. No souls. You got any idea how many girls get killed because they won't come across?"

Johnny didn't have an answer to that.

"So I bothered your actor a little. But he had an alibi and we checked it out and it held up. He was up at his folks' place in New Rochelle getting some stuff together for the trip. He didn't get back to the city until two-thirty or so and he was away from dinner-time on. Which probably puts him in the clear." Haig cleared his throat. "So we've got no suspects for the time being. The rest of your cast managed to give a fair accounting of their time. I want 'em all to stay in town."

"They will. We're staying put for the next two weeks at least, so I can find another actress."

"Good." A long sigh came over the phone. "You just have to grind and grind until something gives. You pick up all the bits and pieces and after a while some of them add up to something. I should have been a shoe salesman.

It would have been a whole hell of a lot simpler." Another sigh. "How about you, Johnny? Come up with anything? Remember any little point you didn't think of last night?"

Johnny considered. He knew something, all right. And he could probably tell Haig about the conversation with Jan without tipping the whole story to the newspapers. Still, first he wanted to meet with the cast and find out what was going on. If nobody else had gotten a call it might be just a false lead that would tie everybody up, a waste of everybody's time.

No, he would not tell Haig. Not yet. Nothing would be lost by waiting, and in the meantime Haig might find the killer on his own.

"Johnny? You still there?"

"Uh-huh. I was trying to think. Nothing new as far as I know. I've been either sleeping or on the phone since I saw you." He drew on a cigarette. "And I only had five hours sleep," he went on, "so I'm not functioning properly yet."

"I feel sorry for you," Haig said. "Only five hours. I haven't been to bed yet. Cops have a soft life, Johnny. And they're all overpaid. The Harris kid gave us a vague line on a few of Elaine's friends. She hangs out—hung out—with a pretty strange crew of Village types. Girls who don't comb their hair and boys who don't shave. I think they call them beatniks this year. Every year there's a new word."

"She would have outgrown it. She was young."

"Yeah. But she didn't get the chance. Anyway, we know who a few of her friends are. A girl named Sin Cardamine. It's supposed to be short for Cynthia, I think. Boys named

Jerry Linden and Lee Sandow. I should be out looking for them right now, asking pertinent questions, figuring all angles. But you know what I'm going to do instead?"

"What?"

"I'm going to sleep," Sam Haig said. "I'm going back to my place and I'm going to sleep. Cops are lazy bastards, Johnny. I've only been up for twenty-six hours. They ought to throw me off the force."

Chapter Four

At three o'clock in the afternoon, Ernie Buell called. He wanted to know why in hell they had to have a stupid meeting that night and why in hell the damned show was being delayed and why in hell some girl wasn't being auditioned for Elaine James' role. Johnny counted to ten twice, reminding himself that the director was a genius and had to be tolerated, before explaining gently that he would get the answers at the meeting. Buell was not mollified, but careful verbal handling managed to soothe his pride a bit—at least long enough for Johnny to get rid of him.

At three-thirty Carter Tracy called. The actor's voice was firm but Johnny could detect suppressed urgency behind the words.

"I have to talk to you," Tracy said. "A few problems have arisen lately, Lane. I'd like to give you a run-down on them and I don't want to go into detail over the phone."

"Something to do with Susie?" Johnny asked. Susie was the character Elaine James had been scheduled to play. If Tracy had anything to say that could not go over the phone, that would simplify things.

"More or less."

"Can you save it for the meeting?" Johnny asked. "There may be a few developments tonight."

"I wouldn't want to raise the point at the meeting."

"Then we can get together afterward," Johnny said smoothly. "If that's all right with you."

"I guess so," the leading man said dubiously. "It's at eight tonight at Jan's place, isn't it?"

"That's right. Want the address?"

"I've been there," Tracy said.

After he had hung up, Johnny mulled over Tracy's last line. He had sounded a bit smug about it, Johnny thought. And he didn't really have much right to. One hell of a lot of men had been to Jan's apartment.

Johnny frowned. This should have made her less desirable, he thought. When a girl has been had by half the world—the male half—it's no great source of triumph to get her into the rack. But somehow Jan seemed more desirable than ever, at least to him, no matter how much mileage she had on her.

Maybe it was the fascination of a mechanic for a highly complex and inordinately efficient piece of machinery. He wasn't sure. But he had a strong hunch that the sensuous brunette was going to be on his mind for quite a while. If on nothing else.

The other telephone call came at a quarter to five.

Ito was near the phone when it rang. He picked it up and Johnny waited patiently while his face took on a puzzled cast. Then Ito covered the mouthpiece with one hand and turned to him.

"It's for you," he said. "But I don't know who it is. Whoever it is, they aren't saying."

"Man or woman?"

"Neither," Ito said unhappily. "Or either. The caller whispers softly and strangely. Are you out?"

"Hell, I might as well take it." He walked to the phone and took the receiver from Ito, held it to his ear. "Hello?"

"Mr. Lane?" The voice was a whisper, a whisper that seemed to be coming through a handkerchief stretched over the mouthpiece of the phone. It was impossible to tell anything about the caller from the voice.

"Who's this?"

"That doesn't matter," the voice hissed, sounding like a snake moving quickly through tall dry grass. "You should abandon plans to produce *A Touch of Squalor*. Drop it cold. The James broad got killed because she wouldn't take a hint. The same thing could happen to the rest of the cast. It could happen to you."

There was a click and the line was dead.

Johnny stood staring at the phone for a long moment, then slammed the receiver into the cradle. Ito looked at him, saw the expression of fury on his face, and quietly left the living room. Johnny paced the floor, his hands plunged deep into his pants pockets, his head down and his eyes blazing.

The nerve of the bastard! Or of the bitch—it could have been either a man or a woman on the phone. The whisperer, whoever he or she was, had done a good job of camouflaging his or her voice.

Johnny lit a cigarette, took two hurried drags, then stabbed it out in an ashtray. It certainly looked as though Jan was right. Somebody wanted to bury the show before it got going. Somebody who cared enough about it to kill.

But who, for the love of God? And why?

He threw himself down into a chair, lit another cigarette and tried to concentrate. What kind of person would want to stop a show?

Backers, of course—if they were convinced their investment was a bad one and wanted to salvage as much as they could. But no one backer of *A Touch of Squalor* had enough money in the show to drive him to such desperate measures, it seemed to Johnny. Besides, the show was a sure-fire moneymaker. And he knew each of the major backers personally, which killed that possibility as sure as Cain killed Abel. And as surely as somebody killed Elaine James.

Johnny took a deep breath. An actor might want to get out of a play under certain conditions. If he had a better offer, a shot at a high-paying Hollywood contract or something of the sort. Or if he had a chance to grab a better play with a probable longer run.

But that did not fit here, Johnny was sure. If any of the cast members wanted out, all they had to do was say so, and they knew it. And nobody in the world was enough of a damn fool to commit murder in order to break a contract. Breach of contract was simple enough in the theatrical world. An actor asked to be released. If refused, he walked through the part like a zombie until the producer had enough sense to fire him and find somebody else to take his place.

And besides the entire cast was excited about the show. Or at least they had been—until the murder. God knows how they feel now, Johnny thought. They were probably scared witless. And he didn't blame them a bit.

He gave up. There wasn't much point to worrying about it anymore. All he was proving to himself was that there was not a single reason in the world for anyone wanting to stop the show.

Yet somebody did.

"I'm going to have dinner out," he told Ito. "Then there's the cast meeting at Jan Vernon's apartment. I'll be eating at McNair's. The number there and Jan's number are both in my book. If anybody calls, you don't know where I am, you're just the properly inscrutable creature of the mysterious East."

"*Master Johnny-san out. Not tell miserable servant where.* Then I call you and tell you what's up."

"Look, if you've got anything doing you can take the night off and I'll let the answering service play my games for me."

"I'd rather have tomorrow off," Ito said. "I've got a tentative date with a Japanese exchange student at Columbia. I was going to impress her with my command of the English tongue." His leer was not remotely inscrutable.

"Besides," he added, "there's a Charlie Chan movie on the late show. It ought to be good for a laugh."

* * *

McNair's was an anachronism. A carry-over from the days when Broadway was a *grande dame* instead of a tarnished neon whore, the ancient restaurant looked all the better for the patina the years had left on her. McNair's was a man's restaurant; the steaks and chops were man-sized and the chef did not waste his time on fancy salads or elaborate desserts. Soft-spoken old waiters in neat dinner jackets padded silently on the plush carpet. Beer was served in pewter mugs, drinks in heavy glasses. Tables were set far apart and high ceilings let conversational noise drift away from one's ears. A man came to McNair's not to mix or mingle, not to see or be seen. He came because he wanted a good hunk of meat cooked properly.

Johnny was starving. Moe, the headwaiter who had been a permanent fixture at the restaurant longer than Johnny had been alive, gave him a smile and a handshake and a table. The waiter brought him, in turn, a double bourbon and a thick blood-rare sirloin with a baked Idaho to keep it company. As far as one Johnny Lane was concerned, there was nothing in the world like steak to take your mind off your troubles. There was a bad moment at the beginning when the knife blade cutting easily through the tender meat reminded him of a razor blade slipping through a tender throat, and that was almost enough to make him lose his appetite. Almost but not quite.

He dug in. And a whole host of problems ceased to exist for the time being. Elaine James was forgotten, threatening phone calls were forgotten, life glowed magnificently. Soon the steak and potato had vanished. The waiter, a master at guessing a customer's wants, came around with a snifter of brandy and a tray of cigars. Johnny inhaled the warm aroma of the brandy, bit off the end of a cigar and lit it with a wooden match. He sat back and poured himself a cup of coffee from the pewter coffeepot on the table.

He was a picture of genteel satisfaction. His suit was sharp enough for Broadway and refined enough for Sutton Place. His shoes were shined, his tie knotted neatly, his hair combed. With the cigar between thumb and forefinger of one hand, the brandy snifter in the other, and the steaming coffee at his elbow, he looked as though he had just stepped out of an advertisement for a brand of expensive liquor.

"I was hoping you'd be here, Lane."

He looked up at Carter Tracy and the mood of contentment shattered like a pane of glass during a bomb test. In slow, measured syllables he damned Ito to eternal hell.

"Don't blame your butler," Tracy said. "He wouldn't tell me a thing. I don't think the fool speaks enough English or has enough brains to tell anybody anything, as far as that goes. No, I came out hunting for you on my own. You're a creature of habit. There are only a few restaurants you go to regularly and this is one of them. That's all."

That, Johnny thought, was all. Silently he forgave Ito and transferred the sum total of his anger to the aging star. The interruption was bad enough, especially when it was by a man you didn't like. But when the guy had the nerve to boast of his skill in lousing up your dinner . . .

"I had to see you," Carter Tracy went on. "It's this messy business about Elaine."

Messy was the word, all right.

"I'm in trouble," Tracy said. "Bad trouble. That's why I had to see you."

"You got a phone call?"

The actor was momentarily startled. "Call? No. Why?"

"Nothing. Go on."

"This is hard to begin. Let me just plunge into the middle of it, Lane. I was with the girl last night. With Elaine."

Johnny's mouth dropped open.

"No, I didn't kill her," Tracy said quickly. "God, I hadn't the slightest interest in hurting her. Quite the opposite—she was so good she virtually assured the play's success. And you know how important that is to me. I didn't sign for this show because of a monumental attraction for the bright lights of Broadway. I'm not interested in legitimate theater, Lane. I'm using *Squalor* to improve my potential in Hollywood. You understand that."

"Then why tell me all over again? You made your point when you signed for the role."

Tracy lowered his eyes. "I saw her last night. I was with her from nine until eleven. It was so innocent it was disgusting, Lane. We just ran through some lines together, got a little of the feel of our parts. That's all."

"If you got out of there by eleven you should be clear. The autopsy placed the time of death between twelve and twelve-thirty. That gets you off the hook, doesn't it?"

"It would if I had an alibi." The actor grinned mirthlessly.

"I was in a variety of bars. I went from one to the next and I got a heavy load on. I don't remember the names of the damned bars and I'm sure no one remembers me. So that puts me right back on the hook again, doesn't it?"

Johnny frowned. "Wait a minute. Haig told me he talked to the whole cast and everybody had an alibi. If you—"

"I fed him a line. I told him I was at a party with some friends, then called up the friends and fabricated a party. If he checks carefully the whole story collapses."

"Why, you fool!" Johnny stared, unable to believe what Tracy was telling him. "You're cutting your own throat. The cops wouldn't have had any reason to suspect you. You're not the first guy who can't prove on the morning after where he was the night before. But now you're setting yourself up for a murder charge."

"You don't understand."

"Don't I?"

Tracy shook his head. "That's not how they'll see it. I have a reputation for seduction, Lane. I'm not boasting. I didn't ask for the damned label. Well, here's this sweet and simple young thing who's playing opposite me. I tried to get her into the sack and she wouldn't cooperate. Maybe she teased me along, then changed her mind. So I killed her."

"That's fine. Except it doesn't make any sense."

"Why not?"

Johnny sighed impatiently. "Because that's an impulse killing. And who the hell carries a straight razor on impulse? I'm sure you don't and I'm sure you didn't pick one up from a bedside table because I don't think Our Girl

Sunday kept one handy so that her boyfriends could slit her throat. So—"

"What did I know about a razor, for God's sake?" Tracy was practically shouting. He closed his eyes, controlling himself, and went on at a lower pitch. "Your cop friend told me she was dead. That was all. Then he asked me where I'd been. I didn't know how the hell she died. For all I knew she'd been beaten to death with a tent stake and I was Suspect Number One. I picked the nearest alibi out of the nearest hat and handed it to him."

Johnny thought about that. It made sense. Tracy's reaction, he supposed, was a logical one—even if it was going to make things rough for him now. Johnny looked at his watch and stood up, stopping to put bills on the table to cover check and tip.

"Where are you going?"

"We've got a date," he told Tracy. "There's a little party over at Jan's apartment. It's called for eight and it's a few minutes after eight already. We'd better get over there as fast as we can. It doesn't do to keep a lady waiting."

"Are you out of your mind?"

"I don't think so. Why?"

Johnny stood watching Tracy's face turn slowly purple. The sight was an enjoyable one. He wondered just how purple the face would get before it split open. It would be interesting to watch. And it couldn't happen to a nicer guy.

"Lane—"

Johnny smiled. "Something the matter?"

"You can't leave me in the middle of the air, damn you! I won't let you."

"I'm not leaving you," Johnny said. "I'm taking you with me. Shake a leg, will you?"

"Do you actually think I've got time for a damned meeting with the police ready to look for me any minute? You can take your silly meeting and—"

It had gone far enough. "Relax," Johnny told him. "Relax before you die of a stroke. You're not as young as you used to be, you know. Quit worrying about the police. I know damned well you didn't kill Elaine. They'll know, too, as soon as I tell them. So don't worry about it."

Tracy's eyes widened. "But—"

"And this meeting is important," Johnny went on. "The son of a bitch who killed Elaine isn't through. He's giving the cast a whole lot of trouble. Unless we get organized he may kill another one of us, or two or three." He smiled pleasantly. "Last night it was the female lead," he went on. "You're the male lead. I suppose that puts you next on his list. Coming, Tracy?"

Chapter Five

There is one definite advantage in arriving late at a gathering, Johnny Lane told himself. Instead of waiting for people, you let them wait for you. You don't waste your time—they waste theirs, which is fine. Thus did he rationalize the fact that the entire group was suffering from the jitters by the time he arrived with Carter Tracy at Jan's apartment.

Stan Harris and Reuben Flood sat on a low-slung modernistic divan set along the far wall of the living room, with Harris looking lost and Flood looking unhappy. Johnny guessed that the little interlude with the police had done nothing to set Stan at ease. As for Flood, his unhappiness was a predictable sort of thing. He was a good, overtly friendly man, a man who felt things deeply. Anyone's death disturbed him profoundly. When a beautiful young girl was murdered, a girl in the same play, you could not expect him to bounce around giggling like an imbecile.

Johnny watched Jan disappear with his and Tracy's coats, her pert little behind twitching impressively, her hips rolling like a boat in rough water with every step she took. His eyes followed that happy sight as long as they could, then veered to study Ernest Buell, who was advancing on him with a drink in his hand and an expression of total annoyance on his face.

"You've got a hell of a nerve," Buell snapped. "Waste my time with a meeting, then waste more of it by showing up late. I need this show like I need a third head, Lane. I—"

"Take it easy, Ernie," Johnny snapped. "You're just sore that you weren't the last guest to arrive. Now sit down and cool off. Everybody sit down. This is important."

Johnny paced the floor in the middle of the room, studying all of them, looking from face to face. Ernie Buell remained belligerent, Flood sad, Stan Harris bewildered. Jan was curled up in a chair, her legs crossed, her eyes dancing. She seemed pleased that she knew more about what was going on than the rest of the cast. She was still wearing the tight black sweater he had seen her in that morning, but she had abandoned the skirt for a pair of skin-tight pants the color of a fire engine. They fulfilled their function, fitting her like her own skin—which, obviously, fitted her very well.

Tony Foy sat alone, eyes bright and alert. Carter Tracy leaned against a doorway and Johnny was willing to bet that the doorway led to a bedroom. Tracy was the type to pick a bedroom door when he wanted a place to lean.

The stage was set. "Okay," Johnny said. "Last night Elaine James got it in the neck, and literally. Somebody slit her throat with a razor. I was the first person to find the body and she didn't look very pretty."

"If I wanted to know that I'd have read the papers, Lane."

Johnny's eyes told Buell to shut up. Then he went on.

"What you wouldn't read in the papers is a little more important. It looks as though Elaine was killed for a reason. The reason concerns every person in this room. She was killed because she was in this show. In *A Touch of Squalor*."

He took out a cigarette and lit it, watching the reactions. Foy and Harris remained expressionless. Reuben Flood started, then got control of himself. Ernie Buell's face dropped.

"Anybody get a phone call today?"

Buell and Flood reacted again.

"A special sort of phone call, I mean. One telling you to get out of the show or get your head handed to you. A threat, that is."

"I did," Flood said.

"Today?"

"Early this morning. Somebody whispering. The call came before—before the police told me about Elaine. I didn't know what to make of it. I—I still don't."

"Neither do I, Ruby. Jan's been getting calls like that lately. And it looks as though Elaine was getting the same kind of calls—before she was murdered."

Ernie Buell got to his feet slowly. "God in heaven," he said, reverently. "I'm sorry, Lane. I got called twice this afternoon. I figured it was some clown who read about Elaine and who decided to have a little fun with me. I thought, hell, it's not enough I have to take some quickie replacement and make an actress out of her, I also have to have a pest on my neck. So I took it out on you. But it looks as if this is more than a pest."

Johnny dropped out of the discussion while the rest of them worked over the same mental ground he had already covered. Obviously they were all scared silly, and they fought their fear by all talking at once. In not too long they managed to establish that (1) they were all in danger, (2) there was no telling who was next on the murderer's list, and (3) it was absolutely incomprehensible that anyone would commit murder to keep *A Touch of Squalor* from opening, or even to want very much to keep it from opening. By the time they reached the point that nothing made much sense—Johnny's conclusions give or take an inch— the room had calmed down a good deal. Johnny took over again.

"This is the way it looks now," he said evenly. "We're in a hot spot. We have a few choices. None of them look too good from here."

"We can't close the show," Ernie Buell snapped.

"Can't we?"

The director shook his head, shortly and decisively. "We've got the right talent here. We've got a package that moves perfectly. If we set it on the shelf now we are very literally burying a play. Burying it! Put *Squalor* aside now and we'll never pick it up again. This is a hell of a play—you all know that, any of you with enough brains to read English. We can't bury a play like this!"

Johnny nodded in affirmation. "I agree with Ernie," he said. "We can't kill the play. We can't get ourselves killed either." He looked at the others. Here and there someone nodded agreement. "I have not mentioned the phone calls to the police. For one thing, I want to keep down the publicity. That's relatively minor. I was primarily concerned with keeping the police off until we made sure the phone calls were really important. I called this meeting when Jan was the only person who had definitely gotten a phone call—as far as I knew. It looks as though Elaine had been called. We can't be sure, but it looks probable. I myself have had a call, and I've found out about two other calls. Even if the caller is a joker, it's time to find out who he is and what he's trying to prove."

"It couldn't be a joker," Reuben Flood said. "Because he knew about Elaine early in the morning. He must have been the murderer."

"That's a point. Anyway, here's my notion. We keep the show alive by means of rehearsals but postpone opening until this bastard gets caught. In the meantime we cooperate with the police. I'll tell Haig about the calls as soon as I get home. He may be able to coordinate the information with something he already knows. At any rate he'll have more to work with and a better chance of getting somewhere."

"So he works on the case while we wait to get our heads cut off?" Tony Foy was standing now, his eyes defiant. "I don't like that, Mr. Lane."

"Got a better idea?"

"Junk the show. Forget it until something breaks. In the meantime, to hell with it."

"And let the mystery voice get what he wants? Just hand it to him on a platter? He'll never get caught that way."

Foy's voice was firm. "I don't care what he wants, Mr. Lane. I don't care whether he gets caught. I just care whether I get killed or not. I say we should put *Squalor* on the shelf. The nearest shelf. It will still be there if we ever want to take it down again."

Johnny listened. There was a hum in the room, a hum like that of an audience after an unexpected speech. He let it ride itself out. Then he said: "You can have back your contract, Tony."

The actor stared.

"You're just a bit in this play, you goddamn fool. You've got a few dozen lines and you want to burn a script because you're afraid there's a guy with a razor behind every parked car. You think he'd waste his time cutting your precious throat? Why, I can walk down any street in the Village and find fifteen guys willing and able to play that part. He wouldn't bother with you." Johnny lowered his voice. "But you can have your contract back. Yeah, I mean it. You'll get it in the mail in a day or two along with a check for what you've got coming. Now get the hell out of here, will you? I have enough trouble already."

There was a silence.

Then: "Mr. Lane..."

Johnny looked at Foy. He seemed younger now. The defiance was gone. The mouth hung weakly, the eyes were unsure of themselves.

"Mr. Lane, may I say that I'm sorry. I talked out of turn, Mr. Lane. I said things I shouldn't have said." Foy forced a grin. "I never thought about getting murdered before. So I overreacted. I want to stay in the show, Mr. Lane."

Johnny nodded to signify acceptance of the apology, wondering as he did so whether both the defiance and the apology had been acts. Tony Foy was a good actor, and most good actors had a tendency to do as much acting off-stage as on. Johnny decided that it did not much matter. The kid had served his purpose. His rebellion and subsequent court-martial had tempered the cast's nerve. They were determined now. The play was to be saved, the police to be consulted, the devil to be given his due.

And on that happy note the meeting ended.

"You cheated me," Jan said.

He had gone to the bathroom, and on the way back she was waiting for him, blocking his path neatly and nicely. She moved forward and let her body lean a little against his. Her head came just an inch or so past his shoulder. He could smell the clean fresh smell of her hair, could feel the warmth of her body.

"You were supposed to come early," she said. "To spend some time with me. Instead you were the last one here. That wasn't very nice of you, Johnny."

"I got tied up."

Her arms went around him and she pressed her body firmly against his. Her breasts were drilling holes in his chest and her mouth was busy at the side of his throat.

"So we'll make up for it," she said. "You didn't get here before the others, so you can stick around after they leave. They'll be going any minute. You can stay."

He dropped a hand behind her and stroked her buttocks. Jan's behind looked very good in the tight slacks. It felt even better than it looked.

She put her lips to his ear and nibbled. "You are going to stay here," she said. "With me."

"I couldn't stay long," he said. "I've got five hundred things to do."

"Not long. Just a little while." She ran her hands over his body. "You're beautiful," she said. "A beautiful man. Stay with me."

"People will talk. It's a little awkward, Jan." Hell, it was damned awkward. When you were on the way back from the bathroom and the hostess practically started making love to you in the hallway . . . well, how much more awkward could it get?

"They talk about me anyway," she said dreamily. Then she straightened up. "You're right," she said. "Look, why don't you leave with everybody else. Then walk to the corner and back again, or something. And nobody will talk."

So she's a tramp, Johnny thought. But what was the matter with a tramp?

"Good idea," he said, feeling foolish, feeling like an adolescent making an appointment for a hot necking session. "I'll leave with everybody else, then take a hack around the block while they all go home. I may be a few minutes. Don't go to sleep."

Her smile was devastating. "Oh, I wouldn't," she purred. "Not without you, Johnny."

Now that, he decided, was known as putting one's cards on the table. Subtlety was not her strong point. So what? Frankness and candor were virtues too, weren't they?

They were, he decided. Especially when they came in such a nice package.

Chapter Six

"Share a cab, Lane?"

Johnny stood with Carter Tracy in front of Jan's apartment building. The other cast members were milling around, either hunting for cabs or preparing for a trek to the nearest subway, depending upon their financial position at the moment. Sharing a cab with Carter, Johnny reflected, was possibly the last thing in the world he wanted to do. "Thanks just the same," he said. "But I've got a few stops to make on the way. I'd better grab my own hack."

"Suit yourself." Carter Tracy's voice dropped to a whisper. "And thanks for dragging me to this little gathering in spite of the way I acted. This is wonderful, Lane. It clears me, doesn't it? Clears me completely."

Johnny nodded noncommittally.

"I'll admit I was pretty stupid," Tracy said, "to hand that police lieutenant a fabricated alibi. But it seemed the only thing to do at the time. I was worried that I'd be in a lot of trouble, Lane. More for lying than anything else. But now that won't have to get aired, will it?"

Johnny looked at him. "What are you getting at?"

"Just that there's no point now in bringing up the fact

that my alibi was a lie. The police won't bother to run it down too carefully, I don't think—not with this new angle to work on. So why tell them about it?"

The man's gall was incredible. Johnny took a step toward the actor, caught his lapels and pulled him up close. "You were one of the ones who didn't get a phone call," he snapped. "Maybe there was a reason. Maybe you were too busy making the calls, Tracy."

"What!"

"You heard me," Johnny said. "You're just a little too worried about that alibi. You're selling me nice and soft but not soft enough. Did you kill her, Tracy?"

The actor's mouth dropped open and stayed that way for a second or two. "That's ridiculous," he managed finally. "And you know it's ridiculous."

"Maybe. Maybe not." Johnny's hand fell and the actor took a step backward. Johnny looked around; the rest of the cast had disappeared. And Jan was waiting inside, waiting for him. "I'm not so damn sure what's ridiculous, Tracy. You're a little too anxious to cover your tracks. So don't tell me what I'm going to give the police and what I should hold out on them. I'll make up my own mind."

A cab came down the street. Johnny held out a hand and whistled. The taxi pulled to the curb and Johnny opened the rear door.

"I think I'll take this one," he told Tracy. "If it's all right with you. I'm in a hurry."

And he stepped into the cab and pulled the door shut.

"Go around the block," he told the driver. "Take it slow and easy, then let me out where you picked me up."

The cabby studied him intently. "Sure," he said dubiously. "You some kind of a nut or something?"

"I'm eccentric," Johnny said. "I'm also a big tipper. Except when cab drivers make themselves obnoxious."

The cabby lapsed into a hurt silence and Johnny settled back to enjoy the ride. It was a quarter after nine—the meeting had lasted a little less than an hour. Haig was probably sleeping, and would go on sleeping for another hour at the very least. For which Johnny blamed him not at all.

But that meant, happily enough, that Johnny could dally with Jan Vernon and feel no pangs of conscience. True, Haig was not the only Homicide cop in Manhattan. But the thought of trying to explain the state of affairs to some officer he didn't know—or some of the ones he did know, as far as that went—did not appeal at all. He couldn't talk to just any cop. It had to be Haig, and Haig was sleeping.

So he would wait for Haig to wake up. And what better waiting place was there than Jan Vernon's apartment?

None, he thought pleasantly. None at all.

The meeting had served its purpose, he thought. If nothing else, it had let everybody know what they were up against. The silent agony that Buell and Flood had been going through must have been enormous. Now, at least everybody knew that the problem was not an individual one but a group affair. Somebody was working on them all together. That wasn't pretty, but at least it drew some of the ends closer together.

Most of the ends remained loose, however, and that was the hellish part of it. He wondered if he might be missing something. Tracy seemed to be the large unknown quantity, and he tried to decide whether the actor could have been the murderer.

It did not work out. Tracy could have killed the girl—but the razor meant it had been done with a motive, not merely on impulse. And no motive had turned up as yet. Or, if you accounted for the razor in some other way, he *could* have killed her on impulse and then made phone calls to divert suspicion, to make the killing look like part of someone else's pressure project. But that still did not work out. Because Jan had been getting calls for a few days prior to the murder, and so had Elaine James. While Tracy might conceivably have killed the girl on impulse, perhaps with some vague motive at the root of it all, he would hardly have taken three days to lay the groundwork.

Johnny shrugged. He thought, maybe I like him for the murder because I don't like him for anything else. But it's better that he didn't do it. Because he fits his part in *Squalor* the way those slacks fit Jan's rear end.

"Hey." The cabby's voice cut through his train of thought and the cab slowed to a stop at the curb. "Hey, character. We're back where we started from. Now where do you want to go?"

"This will do," Johnny told him. The meter read thirty-five cents. He handed the cabby a dollar and told him to keep the change, then hurried into Jan's building.

It was a remodeled brownstone similar in architectural

design to the one he had been in a night ago, the one in which Elaine James had died. The similarity ended with the exterior design. Jan's Gramercy apartment house was plush and comfortable and her apartment took up the entire second floor. There was quite a difference between the two buildings—the difference between a successful actress and one reaching for the big break. All the difference in the world.

He took the stairs two at a time. He stopped at the head of the staircase to light a cigarette. He straightened his tie, drew a breath, and told himself he was supposed to act casual. But he did not feel casual at all.

He knocked. There was the sound of a peephole opening. He stared into it and saw his own face in the one-way glass. Then, happily, the door opened.

And there was Jan.

"It took you a long time," she said. "I was worried for a few minutes. I thought you weren't coming."

"You should have more faith."

"Well, come on inside so I can close the door. Hey, is something the matter? Why are you staring at me?"

"You changed your clothes," he said foolishly. "Again."

"Don't you like?"

"I definitely like."

He liked, all right. She looked magnificently naked, delightfully obscene. She was not really wearing clothing at all, when you got right down to it. She had on what he would describe as peekaboo panties, consisting of a strip of black string around her belly from which a bright red fringe dangled to the tops of her thighs. Her bra was a fringe that matched the panties and was every bit as flimsy. It gave no support, which obviously she did not need in any case. Nor did it do anything to conceal her flesh from his eyes. It just managed to appear sexy, which was its mission.

On top of this she wore a bolero jacket that fell almost to her waist. But it might as well have been cellophane, it was that transparent.

Obviously, her clothing was not meant to keep her warm. But it was sure as hell keeping Johnny warm.

"Classy it's not," she said. "It's vulgar, actually. Common and cheap and all that. They call it French underwear and sell it to peasants and amateur whores and fetishists in the garbage shops around Times Square."

"I repeat," he said, "I like it."

"So do I. It's so blatantly obvious. Does it make me look sexy?"

"You'd look sexy in a rain barrel."

It was true enough, he thought. The dark-haired actress literally oozed sex from every pore. And with her in that outfit, he could see all the pores.

She leaned at him and he took her in his arms. Her body was warm against his, her breath coming fast and hard. He tipped her face upward and kissed her. She threw both arms around his neck and the kiss turned into a four-star production.

"Johnny," she moaned. "Johnny."

He kissed her again and her loins ground into his. As the

kiss sustained, his hand went under the sheer bolero and fondled her back. Her skin was warm and velvety.

"Johnny," she said softly. "What should we do now? What do you think we should do?"

His voice was hoarse. "I think we should go to bed."

"Now that's a good idea," she murmured, nuzzling him. "That's a wonderful idea. Hurry, Johnny!"

They were lying back on the bed, sharing a cigarette and looking up at the ceiling. His heart was beating normally again and he could breathe regularly. There was a silly grin on his face which stubbornly refused to go away, but outside of that everything was perfectly normal.

And she was wonderful.

"I'm not frightened now, Johnny."

He passed the cigarette to her. She took a deep drag and let the smoke out slowly. He watched the end of the cigarette glow when she drew on it. Then he took it from her and smoked.

"I was frightened all day," she went on. "I don't want anybody to kill me, Johnny. Is that silly?"

"Of course not."

"I was frightened. So frightened. And I needed you. The fear must have had a lot to do with it. I wanted you this morning, at your apartment. You were barely awake and I wanted to take you back to bed. You could tell, couldn't you?"

He didn't answer. He thought about the sweet small

sounds she had made while they were making love, about the delicious warmth of her spectacularly female body. Her reputation did not matter now. You could not judge her as you judged other women. She was a special creature, a creature built solely for love.

Which was enough.

More than enough.

"I wanted you all day long. I sat around with the door locked and I worried and wanted you all at once. I thought maybe you would get here early and we could . . . Do you see how shameless I am, Johnny? I wanted to knock off a quickie before the rest of the cast got here. Demure and ladylike, aren't I?"

"You're wonderful," he said. He squashed the cigarette in an ashtray on the bedside table, then rolled over on his side and took her in his arms. His hands stroked her forehead, her cheek, the back of her neck.

"Wonderful," he repeated.

"Sure. Wonderful Jan. A fine specimen of the female sex carried to its logical conclusion. A gal who reacts to any kind of tension by leching for the first man she sets her eyes on. A girl who thinks with another part of her anatomy instead of her brain."

"I like that part of your anatomy."

She didn't laugh. "I'm a tramp, Johnny. Period. I'm a good actress and a good lay and that's all I'm good for." She sighed, then moved away from him. "You'd better get going, Johnny. You have to call that policeman. Craig?"

"Haig."

"Go home, then. Call him and tell him all about it. Get the police working on it so that they can catch the murderer and we can all relax a little."

He sat up on the edge of the bed and fumbled around for his clothing. "I'll tell Haig to take his time," he told her. "I'm in no hurry to catch the killer."

"What?"

"Let him roam around for a few days," he went on. "You see, you're a lot of fun when you're frightened. One perfect hell of a lot of fun."

Her voice was soft. "I don't have to be frightened to want you, Johnny Lane."

"No?"

"No." A soft chuckle. "You can drop around any time you want. You're nice to have around, Johnny Lane."

When he was dressed she wrapped herself in a bathrobe and walked to the door with him. "I want to be able to lock this after you," she said. "I'm still a little nervous, I guess. At a time like this I'm glad I don't live on the ground floor. And that there's no fire escape handy. I used to worry about what would happen if there were a fire. Now I have other things to worry about, don't I?"

He told her to keep the door locked and not to let anybody in. "Even if you know them," he said.

"At this hour?" She pouted. "I wouldn't let anybody into my apartment at night, Johnny. It's after ten o'clock. What kind of a girl do you think I am, anyway?"

"A nice one," he told her. He kissed her and she clung to him for a moment, then let him go. He opened the door and closed it after him, waiting in the hallway until he heard the click of the bolt sliding into place. Then he walked buoyantly to the stairs and down to the first floor.

The night had a cold edge on it. He stood in the doorway and buttoned his coat to the neck. He took out his pack of cigarettes, shook a cigarette loose. He scratched a match and lit it, then stepped out of the doorway.

"Lane—"

He turned at the voice. He had just enough time to see a broad, dull forehead and a pair of piggish little eyes. Then a hand the size of a leg of lamb slammed into his chest. He went down.

Johnny came up fast and hard. There were two of them, one bigger than the other. They wore rough working clothes and heavy boots. The bigger of the two was the one who had hit Johnny, and that was the one he went for. He brought up an uppercut from the floor and threw it at the guy's jaw.

It didn't seem to have any effect. And then Johnny caught another punch over the heart and went down like a sack of oats. The one who had hit him slung him up over his shoulder and carried him to the air shaft at the side of the building. He tried to yell and nothing came out. He couldn't breathe.

The small one—if you could call him small—began to talk.

"Be smart, Lane," he said. "We got a job to do. We got to

work you over. You can have it easy or you can have it hard. You take your choice."

Johnny struggled. But it was not easy to put up much of a fight when you were slung over somebody's shoulder. He wished the son of a bitch would put him down. And then, damn it, the son of a bitch did put him down. Not gently. And Johnny hit the hard pavement like—you guessed it—a sack of oats.

This time Johnny got up more slowly. "All right," he managed to say. "What's the pitch?"

"No pitch. You got a show that ain't supposed to open. We was hired to tell you."

"So you told me."

"But we gotta convince you, see?"

"How?"

The big one hit him again. This time in the stomach. Johnny folded up like an accordion and fell forward just in time to catch a punch in the face. It put him back against a brick wall and he decided to stay there.

A cold, professional beating—that was all. No emotion, no feeling. Just services rendered in return for a fee paid. That was it. And he knew the smart thing to do. You didn't fight back. You stood there and took it and waited for it to end. Then you found a doctor and got him to put you back together. You didn't try to fight your way out of it because these boys were pros and you were strictly an amateur.

Johnny knew all this.

But it was just too cold and mechanical and gut-less for him. Being beaten up by hired machines was too humiliating. So when the next punch came, aimed for the stomach, Johnny slipped to one side and let the fist crash into the wall instead of into his guts. The big one let out a muffled roar and whirled to get him. The smaller one came on fast, going for him with a leather-covered sap. Johnny ducked the blow, spun the guy and left-hooked him in the face. He went to one knee. When Johnny kicked him in the chest he went down the rest of the way.

The big one had a good hand left, which was a shame. He threw it like a shot-putter and Johnny could not get out of the way in time. He hit the pavement with his back, then came up under the man and threw him with a judo toss he'd been practicing. There were advantages in having Ito around, Johnny thought hazily.

But now one of them was behind him and the other in front and there was no place to go. The smaller thug was getting to his feet and the bigger one was already up. Johnny went for the big one—he was blocking the way to the street.

But Johnny never reached him. Instead, Johnny got the sap across the back of his head and the lights went out. His last thought, before the oncoming blackness made thinking impossible, was that maybe he would get lucky and they would not be there when he woke up.

He didn't get lucky.

He came to, a minute or two later, and they were still there. The smaller one talked again. Johnny had trouble hearing the words.

"You had to be cute, Lane. You could have had it soft

and easy but you had to be a hard boy. Now we give more than our money's worth. Now it's gonna be a pleasure to work you over. Maybe we'll do too good a job and kill you. Stranger things have happened."

And then they went to work.

The big one held him while the other one hit him. Hit him in the chest and in the stomach. Periodically the character hit him in the face, too, purely for variety.

It stopped hurting after a while. It became a dull, gray, continuous suffering. At long last the man lowered his fists and hefted the sap.

Johnny could not have ducked the blow if he had wanted to. And by this time he didn't want to anymore. Unconsciousness would be a blessing. His eyes tried to focus on the sap as it came down, ever so gently, against the side of his head just over his ear.

And then the electrician came through with a perfect blackout, and the stagehands supplied a swift curtain.

Chapter Seven

The bed was comfortable. Slowly, carefully, Johnny opened his eyes. It was something he didn't want to do too quickly. You didn't rush a thing like that. A man could get hurt, opening his eyes too quickly. He got them open at last, blinked, saw Lieutenant Sam Haig, and did the only thing possible under such conditions. He closed his eyes again.

"Wake up, Johnny."

Sadly he opened his eyes again.

"Took you long enough," Haig said. "You know what time it is? Two-thirty in the morning. Why is it I always see you at two-thirty in the morning?"

Johnny did not smile. "Cigarette," he croaked.

Haig handed him a cigarette, lit it for him. Johnny's arm hurt when he moved it. His shoulder ached. And his chest felt as though it were held together by adhesive tape. He touched the chest and found out that indeed it was held together by adhesive tape. How about that?

He smoked, ignoring the questions Haig was asking, and his mind began to find the old familiar channels again. He was in a hospital, wasting his time lying in a damn bed.

A pair of hired heavies had put him there. And Haig wanted answers.

Hell, so did he, Johnny. "How did I get here?" he demanded suddenly.

"Quite dramatically," Haig said. "You'll be happy to know that. You came in an ambulance with the siren wide open. Must have hit eighty miles an hour on the way. They thought you might have been seriously injured. Silly of them. It would take more than a blackjack to dent that fat head of yours."

"Who found me?"

"A beat cop. That doesn't mean he has a beard and smokes tea. It means he walks around and kicks drunks out of the way. He went to kick you but he decided you weren't drunk. He called in for help and they checked you into the hospital at a quarter to twelve. You'll live, incidentally. No skull fracture, nothing too serious. A couple of ribs or something are sprung, so you'll have to wear that tape around your handsome torso for a week or so. Who did it, Johnny?"

Lane sighed. "A couple of bozos hired for the job. A pair of heavies from Hell's Kitchen earning spending money. Hell, I don't know who they were."

"You better give me the whole story, Johnny."

He nodded and his head ached. "Yeah," he said unhappily. "I guess I better."

He gave it to Haig from the beginning and the big cop listened without changing expression. Johnny told about Jan's first visit, about the threatening phone calls, about

Carter Tracy's phony alibi and earnest explanation. He explained about the meeting, then gave the details about the beating he had taken in the airshaft next to Jan's apartment building. He left out one scene—the huddle in Jan's cozy bedroom. That, he told himself, was none of Haig's business.

And then he was through talking and Haig was looking at him out of sad eyes and shaking his big head.

"Something the matter?"

"I could never be an actor," Haig said. "Or a producer. Not in a million years. I could never get into the swing of things. I wouldn't fit."

"So? You're a cop. Isn't that enough?"

"It's plenty. And you're a producer, and a good one. And isn't that enough for you, Johnny? Because you sure as hell won't ever make much of a cop out of yourself."

"I—"

Haig did not let him get started. "In the first place, you shoulda called me right off the bat. Soon as the Vernon babe told you about phone calls you shoulda called me."

"I didn't want to send you on a wild-goose chase."

"Let me worry about the wild geese, Johnny. That's just the first place. There's other places. Look, some bright boy wants to close your show. You think it doesn't make any sense. Everything makes sense. Say you've got a mob man who has something against somebody working for you, wants to see him out of a job. Say some heavy has bet big money the show won't open, or doesn't like one of your backers, or anything. You don't have to know the reason, not yet. All you have to know is that somebody has it in for your show. Right?"

"That's as far as I got with it. And—"

"Hang on," Sam Haig said. "I got further than that already. This bastard, this heavy, starts using the telephone. He gives the two girls a hard time because he figures they'll crack easier. He doesn't hurt anybody, doesn't push anybody around. He just makes a few phone calls."

Johnny nodded.

"Next the young one, the James girl, gets killed. Not a case of a beating carried too far. Her throat gets cut open so far you can see her tonsils. And you think the caller did the cutting. That doesn't make any sense, Johnny boy. You don't follow up a vague threat with murder. They take your *Unione Siciliano* card away from you for something like that. So somebody else killed the girl. Somebody who didn't know a thing about any phone calls."

Light was beginning to dawn. Johnny's mouth dropped open. He butted his cigarette and started to sit up.

"Relax," Haig told him. "You beginning to get the message? Is it soaking in?"

"I think so."

"Then tell me about it."

"Somebody killed Elaine," Johnny said. "Then our heavy friend heard about it. He decided to take the credit, figured his threats would be a little stronger with that behind him."

Haig nodded. "And all without any killing on his part. He figures the murderer isn't going to run around waving a flag. He can have the glory all to himself and put on plenty of pressure. It's that simple."

Johnny swallowed. Yes, simple. So simple he would never have thought of it. So simple that it had sailed right past him while his mind had been playing around with all the impossibly complex wrinkles.

He looked at Haig and tried not to resent the slight smile of superiority on the cop's face. Hell, he thought, Haig had a perfect right to feel superior.

"So we're looking for two people," Haig said. "A caller and a killer. Cute, huh?"

"Sure."

"I can't help you with the caller, I'm afraid. That one's going to be tough. But I shouldn't have too much trouble telling you who the killer is."

Johnny stared hard at him. "Give me that again."

"The killer," Haig said. "Hell, you ought to know the answer all by yourself. It's your falling star, Johnny. The aging actor hot for young stuff. He already admitted he was there, then handed me a phony alibi, then told you he couldn't find a real one. He went up there, killed her—"

"With a razor?"

"So he had a razor. Or the lab was wrong and it was some kind of knife. It doesn't matter. He went up there, killed her, came out and got blind drunk. In the morning he woke up with us pounding on his door. He handed us the first alibi that came into his mind, then saw how far that was going to get him and tried a new one on you. He did it, Johnny.

Carter Tracy. Your male lead killed your female lead and it's going to knock hell out of your show."

"I don't believe it."

Haig sighed. "Why—too simple?"

"It just doesn't make sense."

"It makes perfect sense," Haig said. "He already told you one motive. He may have had a better one. We'll find out sooner or later. Murder isn't usually too complicated, Johnny. Nine times out of ten the first suspect is the right one."

"That still leaves one shot in ten."

"Uh-huh. And this isn't that one. There's more, Johnny. I talked to a girl who was fairly friendly with the James babe. Girl by the name of Sondra Barr. One of the pale-lipstick crew from that neighborhood. In fact, Sondra lives in the building just across the street. Seems she looked out the window last night and saw Elaine James walking into her building with a guy. The guy Sondra describes sounds like Carter Tracy."

"So what? He said he was there. Did she see him leave?"

Haig shook his head. "Nope. But that proves he was on hand. And I don't care whether he already said he was there or not. He'll change his story half a dozen times before the jury tells him he's guilty. I'm talking about evidence. Now we can prove he was there."

"But you can't prove he killed her, can you?"

"We will, Johnny."

Johnny lit another cigarette. "I won't buy it," he said.

"But—"

"Listen to me a minute, Sam. You know crime and you

know criminals but you don't know Tracy. I do. I don't like him, but I know him. I don't like him at all. Just the same, I can't see him as a killer."

Haig shrugged.

"You going to pick him up?"

"In the morning," Haig said. "I don't figure he'll run very far. He thinks he's in the clear now, according to what you said before."

"That's what I was getting at. He'll be around in the morning. He'll also be around in the afternoon. Why don't you let it sit on the fire for a few extra hours? Tracy won't run away. And the longer you wait, the tighter case you'll have when you do pick him up—if you ever decide to. Good enough?"

"I don't know." Haig shifted his weight from one foot to the other. His eyes narrowed. "Why?"

"Because I'd rather you didn't pick him up at all."

"We should let him go free so you can put on a show?"

"I don't think he did it," Johnny said. "I think if you wait a while you'll find that out. But if you nab him in a hurry and release him later a lot of things are shot to hell. His career, for one thing. *A Touch of Squalor,* for another."

"He did it, Johnny. You might as well get used to that. He killed the girl."

"I don't think so."

They stared at each other. Johnny watched the play of expression on the cop's face and saw the wheels turning in his mind. "What the hell," Haig said finally. "I suppose it won't hurt to stall till afternoon."

"It won't."

"You going to be busy in the meantime?"

"Probably," Johnny admitted. "I want to see this friend of Elaine's. This Sandra."

"Sondra," Haig said elaborately. "With an *o*. Sondra Barr. It was probably Sandra Barpenschlobber the first time around. What do you want with her?"

"I want to talk to her. About Elaine." He shrugged. "I can't help it, Sam. Maybe I'm too used to plays, where everything dovetails beautifully and the dramatic effect has to be right. Something rings wrong here. Maybe Sondra can tell me something. Hell, I don't know much of anything about Elaine—who she was, what she was like, any of that. She was a good actress and a pretty girl and a virgin and she's dead. That's all I know."

"That's enough to electrocute Tracy."

"Maybe there's more. And I'd like to know about it. Will you hold off on picking up Tracy until three in the afternoon? That'll give me time to snoop around a little."

Haig nodded unhappily. "But you're wasting your time," he said. "You're not a cop, Johnny. You don't think like a cop."

"I'm not trying to be a cop, Sam."

"Hell," Haig said, "I wouldn't worry too much about it. About not being a cop, I mean. Us cops don't live in penthouses. Not even with all the graft we take. Go to sleep, Johnny. I'm going to go collect some graft."

*   *   *

A moon-faced, dull-eyed doctor tried to give him a hard time in the morning. "You need bed rest," he kept saying. "The bones need a chance to relax. We can't be responsible—"

Johnny explained very carefully that he would sign a quitclaim absolving the hospital of all responsibility, that he could take care of his own damn skeleton, and that nothing was going to keep him in bed. The doctor was clearly unhappy but, just as clearly, there was not a hell of a lot he could do about it. Johnny signed the quitclaim, signed himself out, and caught a cab back to his place.

He reassured Ito that he was alive, which was no small task. He washed up, changed clothes, then called Jan and gave her a quick rundown on the beating and the conversation with Haig. "So you can stop worrying," he wound up. "Whoever is trying to send the show up the nearest creek isn't using razors this year. Somebody else killed Elaine."

"And it looks like Carter?"

"That's the way it looks to Haig. Not to me."

"Be careful," she told him. "Very careful. I'll be worrying about you. And Johnny . . ."

"Yeah?"

"You're hurt," she said. "Floating ribs. I won't be able to hug you. We won't be able to . . . uh—"

"We'll find a way," he said. He hung up. It was time to go hunting for Sondra Barr.

Chapter Eight

Sondra, unfortunately, did not answer Johnny's ring. But a neighbor, of whom Johnny presumed to make inquiries, proved quite cooperative.

"Sonny doesn't hang around her pad much," said the neighbor. "You might fall over to the Gila Monster. She makes the scene there kind of regular."

"How do I recognize her?"

"She'll probably be turned on," the neighbor said. He was a young man with a beard that covered most of his face, which was probably just as well. "She's always turned on. So am I, but I'm on a Zen kick. You know—meditation. I turn on to visions of hallucinatory reality."

"That's nice," Johnny told him. "What does Sondra use?"

"Anything. Tea, meskie, hash, juice—she's not particular. So that's how you can recognize her. Which won't help much."

"No?"

"No. Because everybody is turned on at the Gila Monster. It's that type of scene."

It was that type of scene. When Johnny walked in, he

found himself in a low-ceilinged basement that should have been left as a basement, or condemned, or something. The dark, scarred door opened inward. One sealed-up window. Tables and chairs, no two alike, that could once have been furniture on the Mayflower, or maybe on the Ark.

And people. Young men with beards who looked like Actor's Studio types on the skids—torn sweaters, uncut hair, unshaved faces—sprawled over chairs, their eyes shut and their mouths hanging open like caverns. Girls wearing dungarees and sweatshirts and looking most unappetizing, with white lipstick and too much eye shadow. One of the girls had to be Sondra Barr. And, after he had managed to convince the lantern-jawed waiter that he was not a policeman, he learned which one she was. She sat, glassy-eyed and inert, at a small table at the rear. She was alone. He joined her, spoke her name. She looked up at him and her violet eyes were unfocused, blank, opaque.

"My name's Lane," he told her. "Johnny Lane. I want to talk to you."

She did not answer him.

"About a friend of yours, Sondra. Elaine James."

The eyes were still unfocused but the girl came half-way to life. "Elaine's dead," she informed him. "Good girl, Elaine. But dead."

Sondra stared sadly at him. Then, strangely, she began to laugh. The laughter sent chills up his spine. It was sickly dry laughter like the rattle of bones in a dusty graveyard.

"Tell me about her, Sondra."

"The fuzz came around," she said. "Big bad fuzz with a

crooked nose. Showed me a badge and asked me questions. So I told him I saw Elaine with a guy. Fell up to her pad, oh, maybe ten o'clock. Maybe later. Maybe earlier."

He could not help smiling. This, he thought, was Haig's proof. Sondra would be magnificent on the witness stand. She would not even be sure of her own name. A defense attorney would have a barrel of fun with her.

"That's not what I mean," he said. "About Elaine. What kind of a girl was she?"

"Solid. Good to know. What else?"

"Who were her friends?"

Sondra Barr waved a hand that took in the whole room. "Every-body," she said, "and nobody. She was hard to reach. She belonged and she didn't. Like floating."

Like floating? He wondered what cloud Sondra was floating on. "What was she interested in?" he asked. "What was her kick?"

"Ordinary-type kick. She didn't dig getting high. She had this theater bit going for her. She had it almost made before that cat carved her. A bad scene, huh?"

He grunted vaguely.

"And sex," Sondra went on. "That was a kick of hers. Sex is an ordinary-type kick, right, Jack?"

"I thought she was a virgin, Sondra."

The laughter was back again, high and dry and brittle. Then it stopped all at once. "I'm hip," the girl said. "Elaine was a virgin. I forgot for a minute."

"Then—"

"She thought about sex a lot," the girl said. "She had this mystic attitude, you dig? That's all."

He nodded. He was not getting anywhere with Sondra and the place was beginning to get on his nerves. He wondered what would happen if he wanted a cup of coffee. Nobody seemed to be interested in taking an order from him. How did the place show a profit?

"Anything else, Sondra?"

"Hey," she said unsteadily. "Hey, why are you pushing me? Who are you, anyway? Who the hell are you, dad?"

"A friend of Elaine's."

"A friend? Okay, friend. That's all for now. On your way, friend."

"Look," Johnny said. "I was interested in her. I thought she was the greatest. I was starting her on her career, understand? I'm the producer of the play she was rehearsing for, and . . ."

"Producer!" Sondra lost, or half lost, her stoned expression. The violet eyes narrowed, actually focused, carefully measured Johnny as if he had registered on them for the first time.

"That interest you?" he queried.

"Sort of."

"You an actress too? You after a part, is that it?" Johnny figured he might be able to offer her work in exchange for information, in a pinch.

"I'm no actress. I don't want a part. And I have nothing to trade." She was still measuring him with those violet orbs. "Wish I did, though."

"Try hard. Maybe you'll think of something. Why should Elaine's killer get away with it? Let's nail him."

"I'd help you if I could," Sondra said. Her expression went foggy again, and then she seemed to come to a sudden decision. "Would you help me?"

"Sure. How?"

"Well, you're a producer. That means you must make it with the very best chicks. Lots of them. I mean—you know about women. You know how to handle them. Dig?"

"I'm not sure," Johnny admitted.

"Well, Mr. Producer, I'd appreciate it if you would handle me."

It took him a few seconds to get the idea. When it sank in, he said levelly, "For money?"

"Kicks," she said. "Just kicks."

"All right," Johnny said. "But you've got to think of something. I'll do my best to deliver for you—if you do your best to deliver for me. Any little thing. Search your memory."

"It's a deal," Sondra said. "Come on."

She led him out of the Gila Monster and into the fresh air. Now that she was on her feet, he had a chance to look her over.

Pretty good stuff, he had to admit. Tall, and on the slender side. But a beautiful, heavy bosom. A bottom enticingly conforming to the classical pear shape. Long, lively legs. His gaze returned to her face. The cheeks were too hollow. The mouth was too full. But it was an intriguing face, and her hair, falling in red-gold waves to her slim shoulders, was an absolute glory.

This was a deal, he told himself, that could turn out to be a bargain.

He could use a few kicks, himself. And he was pretty confident that she knew more than she had yet told, that in the grip of intimacy she could be persuaded to give him more information about Elaine.

She tapped along on her stick heels, guiding him to her place. Climbing the stairs behind her, he was fascinated by her leg action, gawky yet somehow delightfully graceful, like that of a thoroughbred filly walking up to the post.

Her door was not locked. She just pushed on it, and it yielded.

"Welcome to the pad," she said. She looked up at him out of the foggy violet eyes. "It's true, isn't it? You really do know about women? You really know what to do with a woman?"

"I'd say it was true," Johnny assured her.

She stepped aside to let him pass.

He found himself in a dingy one-room flat, but, unexpectedly, it was neat as a pin. A tailored curtain hung over the one window. The furniture consisted of an unpainted wooden chair, a bridge table, a neat lamp on the table, a small unpainted chest of drawers, and a mattress on the floor. The mattress was neatly covered with a plain brown bedspread. There was no kitchen or icebox. Johnny pushed open a second door, saw a small lavatory. He pushed the door shut. A faint sweet smell, like a whiff of burning hay, came to his nostrils. Tea, he thought. Marijuana.

Sondra walked slowly toward him, the violet eyes wide, misty, and gazing into his eyes with a curious fixity.

"You think I'm turned on," she said. "I'm not. Not very. Had myself a little tea, a while ago, but for me that's not very turned on. So don't be afraid."

"Who's afraid?" Johnny said, the shivers running up and down his spine. Her gaze was like the gaze of a blind woman. Her voice was the voice of a ghost. But she was neat, he reminded himself. Which meant that probably she was clean, also. Then he remembered what she expected of him. She expected him to be a polished, highly competent lover. He reached out and took her hand. It was a surprisingly warm and vibrant hand, not a ghost hand at all. He let his fingers caress her palm.

"Oh, you don't have to force yourself," she said. "I'll take care of that. I know that much."

She danced away from him.

"You just watch me." Sondra laughed shrilly and eerily. "Just watch!"

Johnny sat down on the wooden chair and watched.

Sondra began to strip, making a graceful, fetching game of it. The first move was to lift off her black sweater. As her arms crossed and the garment went up over her head, past the red-gold hair, a pair of generous crimson-tipped breasts came into Johnny's view. Sondra wore no bra. Carefully she folded the sweater and tucked it into a drawer of the chest. Then she straightened up, marched about the room a little, strutting, showing off the breasts. She did not seem particularly proud about them or anything; it was just that she was working on Johnny.

He lit a cigarette, and watched.

With a languorous gesture, Sondra fluffed the red-gold hair. Then she took hold of her loose wool skirt, lifted it, lifted it some more, until the hem rose past her hips. Johnny caught a glimpse of shocking-pink panties before she let the skirt fall.

She moved closer to him. Standing a few inches from him, she repeated the gesture a couple of times, lifting the skirt and letting it fall, lifting and . . .

He reached for her.

She danced away. Standing on the other side of the room, she fumbled with slim fingers at the waistband of the skirt. The skirt suddenly seemed to disintegrate, and slipped to her feet.

She straightened, stood poised for a moment like a lovely figurine, red-gold hair gracefully caressing her shoulders, generous breasts taut and inviting, shocking-pink fluff girding her loins like a ribbon around a piece of candy. Around her hips was a slim garter belt. It held up coarse cotton stockings, black as coal, that made the slim shapeliness of her long legs seem all the more enticing.

She folded the skirt, deposited it on the top of the wooden chest. Then she lifted one of those legs, kicked off a shoe and, bracing herself against the chest, drew off a stocking.

The way she did it was a treat. Johnny's mouth opened as he watched her slender red-tipped fingers roll down the stockings, first denuding one leg and then the other. Twice during the operation she turned her head to smile at him. He felt his heart begin to pound.

She made such a production of removing the garter belt that he found his chair could not hold him. He exploded out of it, as her thumb went inside the waistband of her panties.

"I'll do that," he said hoarsely. "Let me do that!"

"See? I was sure I could excite you, daddy. You dig Sondra now . . . you really want Sondra. Right?"

Johnny answered by taking both her hands and drawing her toward the mattress on the floor. He squatted on it, his head rising as high as her navel. She stood straight and confidently before him as he drew the shocking-pink rayon down over her hips, past her knees and calves. For the first time, he felt the warm, silky skin of her body, breathed in the delicate fragrance of her milky flesh.

"Fold it up," she said.

That was peculiar. To fold a pair of underpants and lay them fastidiously on a chair. Oh, well—neatness. Johnny shrugged mentally, turned back to the mattress and the girl.

It was he who stood now, and she who kneeled. And kneeling, lifting her arms, busying her fingers, she helped him into a state as nude as her own. And then her soft cheek was rubbing itself on his solar plexus. Her hair tumbled along his skin. Her mouth puckered and began to emit small sibilant sounds. It was as if her lips were inviting him, begging him. He flung himself to the mattress, drawing her with him.

And then they went after their kicks.

Both knew what they were doing. Both had been through it before. So they took their time about it. They made the most of it.

They exchanged plenty of kisses in the process. Short kisses. Long kisses. Busy-tongued kisses. But none of them on the mouth.

That did not come until later, quite a bit later. When everything that had gone before suddenly blended and coalesced into a passion that completely possessed Johnny Lane, possessed him and shook him. It was then that they quit playing games. His arms went around her like bands of iron. He did pause to kiss one breast and then the other, sniffing the soft flesh, tonguing the rich nipples. But at last the culmination was at hand. He raised his head, found her mouth waiting, covered her satiny lips with his. Their tongues met, caressed, made love. Johnny's hands were full of her breasts, her luscious buttocks. With a heave, he swung her over. She responded eagerly, hotly, her wet lips clinging to him, her fingers trickling fire.

And then, plunged into the secret darknesses, filling the clutching viscous void, he remembered what she wanted of him. He did not exactly control himself. His blood was too whipped up for that. His every nerve was screaming. But he did manage to preserve his virtuosity, to utilize the skills acquired in the beds of the skilled.

Thus it was that as he climbed to ecstasy, he drew on every device that could carry Sondra along with him. The measured movement, the secondary appassionata of lips and fingers playing their sensual obbligato. Like a rocket, his spirit soared. He rolled and panted, racked by tortures of passion, riding her thrashing legs, lifting on fiery fuel to the skies, the heavens. Then the bomb-burst. In a crashing, blinding detonation of impossible grandeur, Johnny sailed into spasms of rapture, hung suspended for swift seconds on the corners of the universe, then dropped in a long slow arc, like a coasting gull, back to the mattress and to his senses.

He lay still. Sondra lay still.

His nostrils drew in the scent of her hair as he waited for his heartbeat to return to normal.

"Thanks," said Sondra, "for nothing."

"What!"

"I didn't feel a thing. Not a damn thing. Think I'd better go and turn myself on."

Johnny sat up. He was clipped where it hurt, right in his vanity. He tried to pull himself together.

"I don't usually get complaints," he said.

"Not your fault. I never feel a thing—from you male types. See, dad, I thought that if a real smart operator, an experienced guy like you, would go to work on me, I might feel something. But I didn't. No hard feelings."

Still wounded, Johnny sputtered, "I guess our deal is off, then."

"I'm dealing. I just have nothing more to tell you."

"If you knew Elaine, you must remember something. Any little thing."

Sondra sat up too, crossed her hands virginally over her breasts, bit her lower lip with white teeth.

"No," she said finally. "I have nothing to tell you." She sighed. "Poor Elaine. She almost had the bull by the horns. She was going to be rich, you dig? All the money, and no work at all. All the money and hardly any lines to speak. And then someone carved her—" Sondra began to laugh.

Johnny stared at her. Did it mean anything? He stood up, lit himself a cigarette, gave one to Sondra, and started getting into his clothes.

More laughter from Sondra. Then a sudden, sharp break, and the laughter gave way to hysterical tears. Sondra Barr had her face cradled in her arms and was crying her heart out.

Johnny tiptoed out. He knew that he could not help her.

He got the hell away from Sondra's place and the Gila Monster and found a bar, a nice ordinary bar where the customers were quiet, clean-shaven alcoholics and liquor was the only poison used on the premises. He picked out a stool in the rear and ordered bourbon, a double. He threw the shot straight down and passed the glass back for a refill.

Where the hell was he, anyway? Hunting the wild goose with gun and camera, he thought. Chasing down leads that weren't even there, wasting his time and holding up Haig. The lieutenant had already figured things out—Elaine James had been killed by Carter Tracy for one reason or another and everything else was just frosting on the cake, trimmings that didn't alter the basic facts at all. So what was he accomplishing?

Nothing, he answered himself. Nothing at all. It was an ugly gray day in an ugly gray part of town and he had been spending it with crazy kids who had grown up too soon or not at all. That boy, that neighbor of Sondra Barr's. Sondra herself, flying to hell on a fuzzy pink cloud, laughing and crying almost on cue. Maybe it was time to call Haig and scoop up Tracy in the net. Then Johnny could drop the show fast and hard, return the backers' money, and look around for another script.

But something stopped him halfway to the phone. He was not sure what it was—maybe nothing more than a producer's reluctance to bury a package that looked promising, maybe a stupid refusal to accept the obvious. He could still ask a few more questions. There was that boy with the beard, that neighbor.

Johnny went back to the bar, finished his drink and left. He ambled once more to Fifth Street and again walked up the stairs of Sondra Barr's tenement building. He found the apartment where the bearded kid lived and raised his eyebrows at the sign over the door, a sign Johnny had not previously bothered to read. *Abandon All Hope Ye Who Enter Here,* it proclaimed. Quite a switch from a *Welcome* mat.

He knocked gently. "Enter here," a male voice called. Johnny winced, then eased the door open. The boy with the beard—he was about twenty, Johnny guessed, although it was hard to tell because of that chin foliage—was sitting on the floor with his hands clasped behind his neck. His long thin legs seemed tied in a knot, each foot on the opposite knee. The position looked about as comfortable as a bed of rusty nails.

"So you're back," the boy said. "I don't think I caught your name last time around."

"Johnny Lane."

"Lennie Schwerner," the boy said. "Excuse the condition of the pad. It's a mess and I know it. And excuse my not getting up. I couldn't make it. I'm in full lotus posture. It's hard to get in and out of it until you've had a little practice, and I haven't. But it's the best position for meditation."

"You're—uh—meditating?"

"No," the boy said. "Just getting used to the position. You have to be able to sit like this comfortably before you can get anywhere. Comfortable I'm not. You find Sonny?"

"I found her."

"The Gila?"

Johnny nodded. "And on cloud nine-and-a-half. She didn't have a hell of a lot to say."

"So you thought I might," Lennie Schwerner said. "What do you want to know?"

"Anything you can tell me about Elaine James."

The boy whistled softly. "You some kind of fuzz? A plainclothes character? You don't look the part."

"I was Elaine's producer."

The boy nodded vigorously. With his hands behind his neck, it seemed to Johnny as though he were manipulating his head like a puppet. An illusion, of course, but an unsettling one. "That's right," he said. "I remember the name now. Johnny Lane. What can I tell you?"

"Was Elaine a friend of yours?"

"I knew her. A swinging chick in a number of ways. I woulda dug knowing her better. But there was a limit to knowing Elaine. You couldn't get too close."

"You mean sex?"

Schwerner chuckled. "You could put it that way," he said. "She was like stacked, man. So I gave her a try—oh, maybe three months ago. She wasn't having any. She didn't have eyes much for men."

"Sondra told me that Elaine had a mystic attitude toward sex."

"*De mortuis,*" the boy said, "*Nil nisi bonum,* and all. I guess Sonny knows more about it than I do. About Elaine and sex. I guess she does."

Johnny lit a cigarette, offered one to Schwerner. The boy shook his head. Johnny wondered where he was getting. Well, the kid was communicative at least, even if most of what he said did not shed too much light on anything. Hell, he seemed a bright enough lad. Even quoted in Latin. What was he doing living like a bum in a Lower East Side dump?

"Sondra—Sonny, that is—said one thing that didn't add up. She said Elaine was planning on coming into a lot of money soon. I thought Elaine meant she would be making money from the show but I'm not so sure anymore. Sonny gave me the impression that Elaine expected to get the money without working for it." Johnny hesitated. "Did you hear anything about it?"

"I hear lots of things."

"But—"

"*De mortuis*," Schwerner said reverently. "Speak well of the dead. You knew Elaine well, man?"

"Not too well. I liked her. She seemed a sweet kid."

"Then I knew her a little better. I liked her, too. But she wasn't a sweet kid, man. She was too hungry, too anxious. She was—" He broke off and hung his head. "She's dead," he said heavily. "And this is a hell of a way to talk about somebody who's dead."

"Go on."

"Look, I liked her too. You dig? But she was a grasping little bitch. She liked to brag—that's how I got the word on a thing or two. She was figuring on the big payoff, like you said. And not from the show gig. She was looking for hush money."

"Blackmail?" It astounded Johnny. "That—that child?"

Schwerner nodded. "Blackmail. She had a shakedown working on somebody in your show. Don't ask me who. But whoever it was had something to hide. And Elaine wasn't the type of chick to pass up a scene like that. She was gonna milk it for all it was worth." He sighed. "Which was plenty, according to her. She didn't mention numbers but she wasn't talking about nickels and dimes. She meant long bread."

And, to Johnny, that added up. The one stumbling block up to that point had been motive. Carter Tracy wouldn't kill the girl just for the hell of it, or just because she had been holding out on him sexually. It wasn't logical.

But if Elaine were a blackmailer and Carter Tracy were

the fish on her line—that gave him a hell of a good motive for getting her out of the way. Johnny wondered what she could have had on the guy. It didn't matter, of course. It could have been anything. Almost everybody in show business had a skeleton in his closet. And a type like Tracy, hardly staid and respectable to begin with, must have had some dandy bones in with his suits and jackets.

And evidently he had had a razor as well. A razor properly sharp, perfect for opening Elaine's throat and letting her life seep out.

"Like I told you something, huh?" Schwerner's eyes were bright. "You got away from here for a minute, man. You were tuning in to some other station. Does that help any? The bit Elaine was pulling?"

"It helps," Johnny told him.

"Solid. And now you know who did it?"

Johnny nodded. "Yeah," he said. "Now I know."

"Like on television?"

Johnny nodded again. "You've been a help," he said. "I guess I'll leave you to your Zen kick now. What's that position you're in again?"

"The full lotus posture. Why?"

"Just wondered," Johnny said. He hesitated, choosing his words carefully. "Look, I've got a very square question to ask, if it's a big bring-down just tell me to disappear. Okay?"

"Try me."

"Why?" Johnny asked.

"Why what?"

"Why all this? You're not some kind of nut. Your mind

works right. Why sit on the floor and make like a lotus? You believe all this stuff?"

Schwerner wrinkled up his face. "Not exactly," he admitted. "There's some sense to it, but I don't swallow it whole."

"Then why play games? Why the beard-and-beat routine?"

The boy thought it over carefully. For a moment or two it seemed that he might not answer. Then he spoke.

"It's like this," he said. "My old man lives up in Yonkers. He's got his own insurance agency there. Dull as dishwater but it pays for groceries and keeps oil in the tank, you know?"

"So?"

"So I'm not a talented cat. I can't act and I can't paint and I can't write. No sense fooling myself. I'm no artist. So pretty soon I'll be selling insurance in Yonkers. I'll find some chick and get married and buy a house and sell insurance to people who don't want to buy it. I mean, what the hell, there's nothing else I'm keyed up to do. So the old man has a good thing going and I'll go into it." He shrugged. "And in the meantime I might as well bounce around a little. The papers call me a beatnik. The cops don't like me. The people around here stare at me like I have gonorrhea or something. I'm not hurting anybody. I stay nice and quiet and don't get in anybody's way. I'm just having a little fun. I figure it's not going to be any big gas selling insurance, and I'll be selling insurance for a hell of a long time, and after that I'll be dead. And that will be for an even longer time.

So the Zen kick and the beat kick are just something to do first. Make sense?"

"Yeah," Johnny said. "Yeah, I guess it does. And thanks."

"I don't turn on," Lennie Schwerner said. "I don't make a nuisance of myself. I don't even get drunk. I'm not a pervert or anything. I'm not a candidate for Bellevue like most of the cats around here. I'm just enjoying myself."

"You could do worse."

"I probably will. I'll see you again, man. In a few years I'll sell you an insurance policy. Take it easy."

Johnny called Haig at Homicide from a drugstore pay phone. The lieutenant's voice was gruff. "Ready to give up, Johnny? Ready to let me pick up your actor?"

"Yeah, I'm ready."

"What changed your mind?"

"I found something," Johnny said. "I talked to that Sondra Barr girl and another neighbor, and I found the motive you were looking for. I know why Elaine was killed."

"Why?"

"Take it easy," Johnny said. "I want to go along for the ride. Tracy lives over in the Village anyway, so you can pick me up. It's on your way, sort of."

"Where are you?"

"Fifth Street and Avenue B. That's—"

"I know where it is," Haig cut in. "It's not on my way. It's not on anybody's way."

"You want to find out why Tracy killed her?" Johnny said. "Or do you want to play pattycake with him?"

An unhappy sigh came over the phone. "You gotta come along?" the cop asked. "You gotta be a cutie about this? You have a real sense of the dramatic, Lane."

Johnny did not bother to deny it.

"There are times," Haig confided, "when I think maybe you've got the makings of a first-class son of a bitch."

"I'll be waiting on the corner," Johnny told him. "Don't take too long."

And he hung up.

Chapter Nine

"With that penthouse of yours," Haig was saying, "you could also have a chauffeur. Buy yourself a nice long Lincoln. Or a Caddy, say. Then hire some monkey in uniform to drive you around. That would make my life easier."

"I don't need a chauffeur," Johnny said sweetly. "Not so long as I have you."

Haig growled. They were sitting in the back of a police car, an unmarked green Plymouth. Haggerty was in the driver's seat. Another cop whose name Johnny had not managed to catch sat beside Haggerty in front. The two of them were silent.

"Okay," Haig said. "I made a special trip across town solely for the pleasure of your company. Now give. You were talking about a motive, remember? Is it for real or are you saving yourself the price of a cab?"

"It's for real."

"So let's have it."

"Elaine James wasn't so sweet and innocent," Johnny said. "She didn't sleep around but she was no paragon of virtue. Maybe virginity is only womb-deep—"

"Get to the point."

"I'm getting there," Johnny said. "Seems she used to shoot off her mouth about coming into a pile of dough without working for it. At first I thought she meant the show—it was a lush part and a big break. But in that case she'd be working for it and consequently the idea didn't quite figure."

"So?"

"So I asked one of Elaine's acquaintances—not Sondra—and it spilled out. Elaine had a line on somebody, someone connected with the show. She knew something, and she figured the blackmail take would be sweet and long." He smiled. "Now you get three guesses who the blackmail victim might be."

"Tracy?"

"Has to be. Now he's got a motive. Now you can pin him down and skin him. You wouldn't have had much otherwise without digging for it. Sondra's your star witness—the gal supposed to prove Tracy was with Elaine—well, let's just say she wouldn't be much of an asset to the prosecution. She's sort of an apprentice junkie. I had to keep reminding her what her name was."

Haig waved a hand. "Doesn't matter," he said. "Tracy's no professional criminal. He'd crack anyway. We coulda picked him up yesterday and wormed the blackmail bit out of him."

"You're welcome," Johnny said.

"Don't get me wrong—this helps, and thanks. The more we know in advance the easier it is to get him to tell us the rest. This way we walk in with motive as well as opportunity.

A nice package all ready to roll. Of course, what we need is a confession. You know how hard that'll be? Not hard at all, Johnny. Chances are his conscience has got him climbing up and down every wall in town already. He's dying to tell somebody but there's nobody to tell. Well, he can tell us. Maybe a good lawyer can sneak him off with second-degree, but we've got him now."

Johnny lapsed into silence. Whoever the whispering voice on the telephone had been, he could have saved himself the trouble. And he had wasted the dough shelled out for Johnny's beating—it had not been necessary.

Because you didn't get too far with a play when the leading man stood trial for the murder of the leading lady. You took yourself a deep breath, and you put the script into an envelope, and you filed away the whole business for future reference. And you tried not to think too much about it in order to keep from crying and kicking your feet like a two-year-old having a temper tantrum.

Such a nice script, too . . .

"Sort of puts a damper on your play," Haig said.

Johnny sighed. "I was thinking the same thing."

"You can't win 'em all, you know. At least you can tell yourself you've been instrumental in solving a murder. That ought to give you some satisfaction."

"I guess so." The green Plymouth stopped short for a stoplight and the driver cursed gently. Crosstown traffic was thick. The afternoon rush hour was getting underway and the cars crawled through the streets like fat water beetles swimming valiantly through molasses. After a long time they pulled up in front of a chrome-and-steel monstrosity that looked out of place on Barrow, one of the quieter streets in the western part of Greenwich Village.

Johnny said, "Tracy lives here?"

Haig nodded. "He's got the penthouse. Not as fancy as yours, I suppose, but what the hell. It's the penthouse."

"Sure. And it's just about Tracy's speed. The prestige of a Village address coupled with all the ugliness of a housing project."

"It looks like a steamboat," Haig conceded. "But it's where he has a penthouse. Ordinary slobs like me, slobs that don't have penthouses of our own, we're easy to impress."

The building had a slightly broken-down doorman who looked homesick for Park Avenue. Haig flashed his shield and they went on past him. The elevator was self-service, but to get to the penthouse you needed a key. Haggerty got the key from the doorman, turned it in the little button marked PH, and the car went skyward.

"Impressive," Haig remarked, "You can't even ride up there without a key. You got a gadget like that at your dump, Johnny? Or aren't you that fancy?"

"You've been there. There's an operator running the car so you don't need a key."

Haig winced. "Suppose you're a visitor at this place. How do you get up?"

"You tell the doorman," Johnny explained patiently. "And he calls upstairs and checks you out, and then he uses his key in the elevator. The one you're holding in your hand."

Haig looked thoughtfully at the key, then shrugged and put it into his pocket. The car eased to a stop and the door opened. They stepped out of the elevator and into the foyer of Carter Tracy's apartment. It was an impressive layout, Johnny had to admit. The furniture was too extreme for his tastes, too modern in design, maybe a little too flashy. But then it had to reflect the tenant's personality, and in that it succeeded admirably. It was just the sort of place Tracy would pick to live in—an over-thick carpet laid wall-to-wall, glaringly daring arrangements of lamps and sectional couches and tables, all too low to serve other than a decorative function for a human being of normal size. Blinding abstract paintings set the walls on fire. It was fine for Tracy, but Johnny could not see how anybody else could stand living in it.

"Tracy!" Haig's voice echoed through the apartment. "Police officers, Tracy. We want to talk to you."

Silence.

"Maybe," Johnny suggested, "he's not home."

Haig turned to Haggerty. "Go down and talk to the doorman," he said. "Find out if Tracy left the apartment this afternoon. Ask him—"

"Sit down and relax, Haggerty." Johnny grinned. "It would be easier to call the old coot on the phone, Sam. Not that one—the intercom. Over there on the wall. Here, let me."

Johnny picked up the intercom phone, jangled the hook

a few times and waited until the doorman got around to answering it. "Police," he said. "Mr. Tracy leave the building since you came on? Uh-huh. Yeah. He have any visitors? Yeah. Thanks."

He returned the receiver to the hook and turned to Haig. "The doorman's been on since noon," he said. "Tracy went out to lunch at one and came back half an hour later. He's been here since, as far as our boy knows."

"Visitors?"

"None. Tracy's here and he's alone. Why don't we look for him? That might make sense."

"Hey, good thinking, Johnny." The tone was mild but the implication was obvious: *Quit showing off, sonny boy. We like you and you've been handy but we know our business. So sit down and behave.*

"Sure," Johnny said. He lowered himself uncomfortably to an uncomfortably low couch and picked up a copy of *Hollywood Reporter* from a low coffee table. He flipped it open and tried to get interested in the not-too-exciting trade gossip of a not-too-exciting trade. If Hollywood would only stop being Hollywood, he thought sadly, they might manage to accomplish something out there.

That train of thought lost him. He turned to the scandal section, a column written by, for and about idiots, and tried to care who was infanticipating and who was headed for Splitsville and what U-I hot property was last seen with what director on the Twentieth lot. He failed. He was reading the latest inside poop—the columnist's word—on the latest heartthrob of a teenage teaser with the improbable name of Thursday Rivet when he heard Haig's voice.

"Johnny!"

He stood up quickly. "Aha! You need my special talents. You've run into a snag—"

He broke off the sentence when he saw the look on Sam Haig's face. The big cop was standing in the doorway of what looked like the bedroom. His shoulders were slumped and his face had a haggard look.

Johnny reached him in a hurry.

Johnny went inside.

He took a good look.

He saw a bedroom, the ceiling high, the walls a bright baby blue, the bed huge and built for comfort. He saw cigarette burns on new furniture, the scars of cigarettes forgotten while the bed was being put cheerfully to use. He saw a set of matched and expensive luggage in one corner, a big picture of the room's tenant on one wall, another glaring abstract on another. He saw two empty liquor bottles and one packet of contraceptives prominently displayed on the dresser.

He also saw a body. The nude body of Carter Tracy. It lay on its back on the bed, lay on the sheet with the bedcovers carelessly kicked down around the foot of the bed. The eyes in its head were open and glassy. Its hands lay palms-up at the sides of its torso.

Its throat had been cut wide open.

*   *   *

There were times when you didn't want to think about anything in the world. There were times when all you wanted to do was to go home to your own place and open one or two bottles and get very drunk. Not happy drunk, which would be impossible. Not moody drunk, which would be unpleasant. Just drunk, dead drunk, so that when you closed your eyes and passed out you would be so thoroughly stoned that you wouldn't even dream.

That was about the way Johnny Lane felt.

"I don't even want to talk about it," Haig said. "I don't want to talk about it or think about it or do anything at all about it. Everything was all set up, everything was perfect, we had the motive and the means and the opportunity, we even had the goddamned murderer. We guessed it right, we figured it right, we saw the whole mess clear through. The leading man killed the leading lady and the ball game was over."

Johnny didn't say anything.

"Then this," Haig went on. "Our killers get killed. The old switcheroo. And the killer isn't the killer anymore, because our killer gets killed the same way our victim got killed. Same position, same set-up, same everything. It's a goddamn grisly joke and the goddamn joke's on us."

Johnny didn't say anything.

"God knows where we are now," Haig said. "I don't need a lab man to tell me we aren't going to get a print we can use out of this place. We've got two murders to solve instead of one and we don't have a reason for either of them anymore. A virgin turns up nude in bed with her throat cut and we look for a killer. Then a satyr turns up in bed with his throat cut and we still look. A goddamn joke."

Johnny didn't say anything.

"For a minute," Haig said, "it didn't look possible. You know what I was thinking? I got this bright idea, this brainstorm. Tracy figured his goose was cooked, he might as well go out in style. So he took off his clothes, stretched out on the rack and drew a line across his neck. You know it took me a few minutes before I got to wondering what he did with the razor. This case is getting to me, Johnny."

Johnny didn't say anything.

"Go home," Haig said. "Call everybody and tell them the show isn't going to happen. Call the papers and tell 'em to print it in the morning. Tell 'em the show is off permanently. Somebody doesn't want your play to go on, Johnny. He's holding all the cards. We can't figure out what his angle is, not to speak of who in hell he is. We'd better let him have his way for the time being. In time he'll slip and we'll hit him. Or her, or them, whatever the hell it is. Go home and make your phone calls and take some aspirin. Or some bourbon. Suit yourself."

Johnny still didn't say anything. He gave Haig a half-nod and left the apartment. He took the elevator downstairs, walked out of the building and over to Eighth Avenue where he caught a taxi headed uptown. His head ached horribly and his ribs were sore—somehow he hadn't really noticed the soreness until now. He closed his eyes and let the cabby fight the traffic.

*   *   *

Johnny was sitting in a soft chair with a glass of bourbon in his hand. The calls—to everybody vaguely connected with the show, to four morning dailies plus the trade papers—had been made by Ito. But Johnny had saved Jan for himself. In a way she'd been on the inside with him from the beginning and he wanted to give her the story instead of passing it on through an interpreter. But he didn't feel up to making the call yet.

"One thing still seem Chinese puzzle," Ito said. "Not see—"

Johnny sighed. "Ito, cut the comedy."

"Sorry," Ito said. "It was that damn Charlie Chan movie. It was funny enough but those things can soak into your system."

Johnny said, "The Chinese puzzle, Ito?"

"Yes. You told me the doorman said Tracy didn't have any visitors. How did he get killed?"

"By a visitor." Johnny finished the bourbon, put the glass down. "One who got past the doorman. That's all."

"Without a key to the penthouse?"

Johnny nodded. "The building has an open staircase," he said. "Every building has. Fire regulations. The stairs reach the penthouse. Tracy's visitor walked right past the doorman, took the elevator to the floor below Tracy's, say, and walked up a flight of stairs. Simple enough?"

"Sure. Same thing going down?"

"Maybe, maybe not. It doesn't really matter. To get down from the penthouse you don't need a key. You ring and the elevator comes up. Then you press the *one* button and down you go. Puzzle all cleared up now?"

"All clear." Ito turned away slightly. "Uh . . . do you want me to stick around tonight?"

"Oh. You got that date with Miss Tokyo?"

"She's not from Tokyo. But her home town is a filthy word in English. She isn't aware of this. Which can be embarrassing. Yes, I have a date with her."

"Then keep it."

"You don't need me?"

"Hell, no," Johnny told him. "If the phone rings I'll answer it myself. If you can fake a Japanese accent so can I."

He waited until Ito had left before he called Jan. When the servant was gone he went into the kitchen and poured himself a cup of hot black coffee, carried the coffee back to the living room and lit a cigarette to keep it company. He didn't want to call Jan until he knew what he was going to do next. And he didn't know what he was going to do next.

He knew what he was supposed to do next. He was supposed to sit on his behind and wait for something to happen. Nothing would happen, which meant he would have a hell of a long wait. The killer—the son of a bloody bitch whose middle name was Razor—didn't have to make a move. He had already gotten what he wanted. Two killings and one beating had turned the trick. *A Touch of Squalor* was not going to be on the boards that season.

But what in hell was Johnny Lane supposed to do? The

killer would get away. He did not have to stick out his neck anymore and he hadn't left any trail behind him. No matter how you figured it, there was no reason for anyone to want the show ruined, no reason for anyone to kill Elaine and then Tracy. Hell, there was a reason—there had to be a reason. But there was no way to figure it out.

He picked up the phone, and dialed.

"Hi, Jan. This is Johnny," he told her. "Anybody call you?"

"Ernie Buell. I heard about Tracy. I thought—"

"That's what we all thought," he said. "I found out something else today. Elaine was blackmailing him, had him over a barrel. That must have been why he was so scared he'd be fingered for her murder. I went over with Haig to pick him up, but somebody got there first."

"And killed him," she said.

"Same as Elaine—a razor slash across the neck. We're closing the show, Jan. We're shutting down while we still have a few people left."

She made no reply for a second or two. Then: "I guess we have to, Johnny."

He nodded. Then he remembered that nods didn't register through a telephone. "Yeah," he said. "Our hand is forced."

"That's the way it looks, Johnny. I suppose the police will get the killer, but—"

"How?"

"What do you mean?"

"How will they get the killer?" he demanded. "Haig is up

against six different stone walls. He hasn't got a single angle to work. I know damn well what he's going to do. He'll let the case move along the regular procedural lines until it gets lost in the files. He'll let it bury itself. You can't solve every murder, Jan. They'll work on this one until it stops turning up in the newspapers. Then they'll forget about it."

"They might get a break."

"Sure they will," he said. "Somebody will get a guilty conscience and turn himself in. Or they'll get an anonymous tip from a disgruntled mistress. But don't hold your breath."

"Johnny—"

"You know what? It's a temptation to write off the whole thing as the work of a nut. A crackpot. Somebody with a cockeyed grudge against the world. Or against the show, I don't know. Some moron who doesn't like the title. Hell, we could have changed the title. Called it *A Touch of Horse*—"

"Johnny."

He took a deep breath.

"Johnny, why don't you come over for a while? I'd like to see you, Johnny. You could relax."

He heard the syrup in her voice and remembered the night before. It had been good then. It could be good again.

"My rib cage . . ."

"We'll be gentle."

He let it hang there for a minute. "No," he said finally. "No, not tonight, Jan. I've got things to do. I may be able to turn up something. I'm going to give it a try."

"What can you do that Haig can't do? You're not a cop, Johnny."

Daylight dawned.

"You're right," he said slowly. "Sam Haig keeps telling me the same thing. I'm not a cop."

"Johnny?"

"I've got work to do," he told her. "I'll call you as soon as I get a chance."

And he put down the phone.

Chapter Ten

The bar was in Hell's Kitchen, that totally unglamorous section of Manhattan where large four-legged rats devour babies in their cribs and where their two-legged counterparts lend money to dockworkers at rates of interest that would have made Shylock wince. The bar crouched on Tenth Avenue between 35th and 36th Streets. A neon sign with a nervous tic announced that the bar was named Sully's Place, and the odor that issued forth when the door was open announced that Sully did not believe in washing the floor. The odor was one part spilled beer, one part urine, and two parts vomit.

The man walked into Sully's Place a few minutes before ten. There were four people inside plus the bartender. Five heads turned lazily to take a look at the man when the door opened; nine eyes—a tenth had been lost in a fight several months before—focused on the new arrival. They took him in at a glance, saw who he was, and turned away instantly.

You did not take long looks at a syndicate man. It was unhealthy. It brought visions of six bullet holes grouped in the precise center of a man's forehead, of cement overcoats and prolonged swims in the Hudson.

And this man was a syndicate type.

That much was obvious. It showed in his walk—hands in pockets, head set back on shoulders so that the neck nearly disappeared, shoulders set and legs striding easily, cockily. It showed in his dress—black Italian porkpie hat with a brim a little too short, black overcoat cut a shade too long and bulging ever so slightly over beside the heart where a gun was waiting, black Broadway suit, slim and highly polished black shoes.

Most of all, it showed in the face. The firm little lines around the mouth. The hawk nose. The slight pouches beneath the eyes. And the eyes themselves—very narrow, half-closed, and staring flatly ahead showing no expression whatsoever.

The man walked past the four customers without looking at them. He went to the far end of the bar. He did not sit on one of the stools but leaned against the bar itself. He drew the bartender without a gesture. His eyes brought the man over.

The bartender was fat. He carried his stomach in front of him like a proud, pregnant woman. He hurried.

"What'll you have?"

The man shook his head shortly. When he talked, the words were pitched so that only the bartender heard them. The lips did not move.

"Some muscle," the man said. "Two boys. Big boys."

"Nobody around here," the bartender whispered. "Just a couple of lushes. You wanta go up the street—"

The man's eyes stopped him cold in the middle of the

sentence. The bartender looked into those eyes and saw Death staring him in the face. He wanted to look away but he could not.

"Information," the man said flatly. "Yesterday two boys did a job."

"There's a lot of muscle jobs."

The man's hand snaked inside his coat and the bartender took an involuntary step backward. The hand came out holding not a gun but a cigar. The man pierced the end of the cigar with a toothpick, then lit up with a gold lighter. The cigar stayed in the corner of his mouth and he talked around it. The bartender almost relaxed, but his hands were still trembling a little.

He did not want trouble. He did not want any trouble at all. And if this man, this fellow from the syndicate, got annoyed, there would be trouble. The bartender operated with the silent permission of the syndicate. If this permission were lifted, things would happen swiftly. His business would probably disappear. His liquor license could well disappear.

He himself might disappear.

"This job," the man said. "Over in Gramercy. Last night. Ten or eleven. A Broadway type got a little push-around. A producer named Lane."

The bartender nodded slowly.

The man shifted the cigar from one side of his mouth to the other. "I want to know who," the man said. His voice somehow hardened without going up or down in volume, without changing tone. His lips still did not move. "I want to know who and I want to know where I can find them. They did good. I might want to hire them."

The bartender's voice dropped from a whisper to a breeze blowing through dry grass. "Lou Rugger is all I know," he said. "Lou Rugger."

"There was two."

"All I know is Rugger," the bartender said. "Big guy with one mitt bandaged. Real big guy."

The man said nothing.

The bartender hesitated. There were some things which you were not supposed to tell anybody, he thought. But there were some people you told whatever they wanted to know. The bartender was in the middle.

"A bar over on Twenty-eighth," he murmured. "The Castle. Either he's there or they know where."

"The Castle," the man said.

"On Twenty-eighth east of Tenth. You ask for Lou Rugger. Or you see him there."

The man did not answer. The cigar moved in his mouth. Then he turned from the bartender and started walking toward the door. No heads turned to follow him.

The man, of course, was Johnny Lane. He did not resemble Johnny at all, however. A careful application of makeup had changed the face, altering mouth and eyes, building up the nose. He wore appropriate gangland clothes. The walk and the voice and all the mannerisms were carefully stylized, the words and phrases meticulously selected.

The effect was perfect.

Sully's Place had been the fifth he had visited. In the

other four his approach had been effective enough but each of the four bartenders had disclaimed any knowledge of the muscle characters who had knocked Johnny around the night before. Sully's Place had paid off. Now all he had to do was walk through the night to the Castle and find Rugger. The rest would be easy.

He passed a newsstand at Thirty-fourth and read the headlines on the first editions of the morning tabloids. Tracy's murder was the lead item, which didn't particularly astonish him. The *News* and the *Mirror* could not ask for a better piece of news. The killing had all the elements of hot copy—a chain murder, related to Elaine's death and following the pattern perfectly; a sex angle, since Tracy was found nude. And a celebrity gimmick—every show-business personality automatically became a celebrity in newspaper parlance once he died violently, and Tracy was fairly well-known to begin with. He had been a star, albeit a falling one.

Johnny kept going. He walked down Tenth as he had walked into Sully's Place, head cocked and shoulders set and hands in pockets. It would have been easier to put on the role when he got to the Castle but he stayed in the part on the way. He did not want anybody to notice him behaving out of character, for one thing. For another, the Method School of acting had a few sound things to say. If you lived a part you played it more effectively.

He turned on Twenty-eighth and found the Castle. The neighborhood was slightly better south of Thirty-fourth Street and the Castle was correspondingly higher in tone than Sully's Place had been. The clientele was uppercaste for the Kitchen—minor loan sharks, numbers runners, ten-dollar prostitutes. He stopped in the doorway to straighten his tie, then took a few steps inside and glanced around. The shorter of the two men who had worked him over a night ago was not there, but he saw the big one, the one Sully had called Lou Rugger. Johnny ignored the man and stepped up to the bar.

Like Sully, the bartender at the Castle came over to him in a hurry.

"Tell Lou Rugger," Johnny said, "that I'm outside. Tell him I want to talk to him."

He did not wait for an answer. He turned around and walked casually out of the bar. On the outside he puffed at what was left of his cigar and waited for Rugger to get the message.

Soon Rugger came out, his face puzzled, and walked over to Johnny. There was no recognition in his eyes.

"You wanted me?"

Johnny nodded. "You do muscle work," he said. "You're for hire."

"So?"

"So maybe I can use you. First we talk. You got a place handy we can talk?"

Rugger thought about it. "Down the block," he said. "There's a building condemned. Nobody there now."

Johnny gave him a look.

Rugger hesitated. "We could go to my place. I got a room around the corner. But my broad's there."

"She could move," Johnny suggested.

"Yeah, but—"

She was probably working, Johnny thought. Working flat on her tail with her knees pointing at the stars. A man like Rugger seemed capable of holding two jobs easily enough. Muscle man and pimp.

"Forget it," Johnny said. "The building's fine. Let's go." The street was dark. He followed the big man down the block, followed him when he turned at a doorway. The building deserved to be condemned. When they condemn a building in New York they chalk huge white X's on the windows. But this particular building had few windows left.

"That's far enough," he said. "Now turn around."

Rugger turned. He started to say something. Then he saw the gun in Johnny's hand. Rugger's mouth fell open and his face went white. Even in the half-light thrown by a street lamp Johnny could see how pale his face was.

"Hey—"

"You die now," Johnny said. "You die, Rugger. How do you want to die? Quick or slow?"

Rugger tried to answer but no words came out of his mouth. He seemed thoroughly lost. Things were happening too quickly for him to follow them.

"You did a job last night," Johnny said. "A muscle job. A guy name of Lane."

"We had orders."

"From who?"

Rugger closed his mouth. That was the code, Johnny

thought. You didn't talk. You took whatever they handed you and you didn't talk. That was why Johnny had to play the role all the way. It would have been a pleasure to drop the part, to tell Rugger who he was and then beat the information out of the big goon. But it wouldn't work that way. Rugger would talk only to somebody who was more of a mob man than the man who had hired him in the first place. And he would talk only with a gun staring him in the teeth—all the beatings in the world couldn't open him up. "This Lane," Johnny said. "He was better connected than you thought. He knows a lot of people."

"I didn't know."

"You know now. So you get hit in the head, Rugger. You get killed."

"Look—"

Johnny was holding the gun in his right hand. With his left he took the cigar from his mouth and threw it to the floor. He covered it with his heel and ground it out. "You'd better open up," he told Rugger. "You better say where the job on Lane came from. You better talk fast."

"Look, I—I don't know who it was."

Johnny flicked off the safety catch. "First I shoot off your knee-cap," he said. "You know how that feels? Then when you fall, I let it go into your gut. Then I give another slug in your . . ."

"Take it easy," the big man begged. Terror gleamed in his eyes. "I'm telling you the truth. I'm not holding out."

"Yeah?"

"I did the job with Marlo. Jackie Marlo—hangs out on Bleecker, around there."

"Go on."

"Marlo don't know more than I do. We got this job—work over this Lane, don't kill him but hit him a little. Enough to put him off doing this show." Rugger hesitated. His eyes dropped to the gun, then came up again. "Yesterday afternoon," he said, "a little kid comes in with a note plus half of a hundred-dollar bill. You know—the bill torn in half, right down the middle. There's a note attached to the bill, says I should stay close to the phone in the Castle. So I do. What the hell—you get half the bill, it's not worth a thing without the other half. And nobody rips a bill for a joke."

"Keep talking."

"I stayed near the phone. Maybe five minutes later it rings and I pick it up. This voice asks me if I got the piece of the bill. I say yes."

"What was the voice like?"

"Like nothing," Lou Rugger said. "A whisper, sort of. A low whisper."

"Go on."

"This voice says how would I like to make the other half of the bill. I say fine, who do I have to hit? The voice tells me about this Lane. I'm supposed to get a call later that night saying when and where." He paused, shrugged his shoulders. "I thought it was a solo. Later I get the call, go over and wait for Lane to show. I run into Marlo—he got the same deal. Half a bill to start, the other when the job was over. We waited for Lane and we worked him over. That was all."

"Did you get your money?"

Rugger shook his big head. "Not yet. So I got half a bill. It don't make any sense. Why should the guy keep the other half? It don't do him any good."

Johnny had to work to keep the smile off his face. "He didn't keep the other half, stupid. He sent it to Marlo."

Rugger's mouth opened very wide.

"So you and Mario got a yard between you," Johnny went on. "If you put the two halves together. You're a jerk to fall for an old one like that, Rugger. And a jerk to work for people you don't know. You get in trouble that way."

"I—"

"Who gave the bill to the kid? Didn't you think of asking?"

The muscle man lowered his eyes. "The kid was in and out before I knew what was coming off. I don't even remember what the kid looked like. The streets are full of kids. They all look the same."

"The second phone call. What time did you get it?"

"Around nine. I don't know."

"And you went right over there?"

"Yeah. We waited around for Lane. He came out alone and we picked him up."

That narrowed it down a little, Johnny thought. It wasn't a complete blind alley. But that was as much as he was going to get from Rugger. The man did not know who had hired him. He could not tell even though he obviously wanted to.

"Look," Rugger was saying. "Look, I got suckered, too. I got stuck on the money end of it. I shouldn't of taken the job in the first place, all right. I needed the dough so I took it. Lay off, will you?"

Johnny raised his left hand, dipped into his jacket pocket. He took out a handkerchief and wiped his face with it. He rubbed makeup from the corners of his eyes, from his mouth. He let his face relax. His posture changed from gangster stance to his usual position.

"Rugger," he said, his voice normal now. "Don't you recognize me, Rugger?"

Rugger blinked. Then recognition came, and shock. The man started to move toward Johnny. Then he remembered that mob man or not, Johnny was still holding a gun in his hand. Rugger stopped in his tracks.

Johnny shrugged out of the heavy coat. He let it fall and stepped toward Rugger. "Now there's just two of us," he said. "Let's see if you're worth a hundred dollars or not."

He dropped the gun to the floor. And Rugger rushed him, coming fast and hard.

It did not last long. Rugger was on his own this time and Rugger was soft from too much beer. Johnny ducked the first punch and came up under it, sinking a right to Rugger's belly. When Rugger folded, Johnny linked both bands behind Rugger's head and rushed the head down into his own knee. The knee was an effective club. It knocked out two or three of Rugger's teeth and brought a rush of blood from his flat nose.

He came up and rushed where angels feared to tread.

Johnny ducked another punch, dodged one that would have cracked his jaw if it had landed. Then he moved inside, pivoted and tossed Rugger into a wall. The wall gave way and Rugger went partway through it. He came up cursing but he came up slowly and most of the fight was out of him.

A left to the jaw finished the job. He went to one knee and stayed there.

"That was a fight," Johnny said.

Rugger was silent.

"We didn't have a fight last night," Johnny told him. "We started off with a fight. We wound up with a beating."

Rugger stared.

"So now you get a beating," Johnny said, hauling the other to his feet. Johnny held him with his left hand and hit him with the right. Rugger lifted into the air. He sagged and fell on his face.

"The building's condemned," Johnny said. "They have to tear it down anyway. So we're saving the wrecking crew some time. We're knocking the walls down for them. You're the battering ram."

He picked Rugger up again. It was like picking up a corpse. He aimed Rugger at a wall and sent him on his way. Rugger took the wall with his shoulder and crashed off in time to get hit in the face once more. He fell down and sat on the floor.

"Get up," Johnny said. "C'mon—get up."

Rugger got up and Johnny hit him again. They went on that way until Rugger could not get up any more. Then all the fun was gone. Johnny rescued his gun, jammed it into the shoulder holster. He grabbed the coat and put it on, set the short-brimmed hat on his head. Then he prodded Rugger in the ribs until the man's eyes opened. "You shouldn't beat up people," Johnny told him gently. "It's a rotten way to make a living. Besides, you can get hurt that way."

Chapter Eleven

Johnny took a cab back to his apartment. That was the best move, he decided. The alternative—hunting for Jackie Marlo on Bleecker Street and handing him the same routine he had handed Rugger—was not entirely without appeal. But in the long run it would be a waste of time, an elaborate game which would only result in his knocking Mario around without getting any additional information. And it could work the other way. If Rugger recovered in time to warn Marlo by telephone, Johnny could get more than he had bargained for. No, the only sensible thing was to go home. There was bourbon there, and coffee, and a comfortable chair. All of which sounded inviting.

The hack took Eighth Avenue. Johnny gazed out to the right, watching the throngs of people pouring out of the theaters along the side streets leading from Broadway. His eyes took in theater marquees: *Up for Grabs—A Sound of Distant Drums—The Lonely.* All good shows, and all drawing good audiences. *A Touch of Squalor* belonged with them, he thought. But it would not be up there, wouldn't place a few more neon jewels in the hair of that tarnished lady named Broadway. Not for another season. Maybe never.

He sighed. Hell, the play was a minor casualty when you stopped to think about it reasonably. The major pity was that two fine actors were dead. One of them happened to have been a son of a bitch, and the other happened to have been a blackmailer, but they had been actors, good theater people. They would have been great in *Squalor*.

And they were dead.

He thought back to what he had managed to learn from Lou Rugger. First of all, Johnny now knew one thing about the killer. He was not a professional mobster as Haig had half-guessed. A gangster type would not have hired muscular talent in such a bizarre manner. If you were one of the hard boys and you wanted muscle you went calling and arranged the deal.

Which meant the killer was an amateur. A clever amateur—it took a little ingenuity to hire a pair of playboys like Rugger and Marlo without letting them know who you were. And letting a single hundred-dollar bill do the work of two was a touch of genius tempered with poetic beauty.

Admirable.

What else did he know? Well, Rugger had said that the joker with the whisper made his last call around nine. That was roughly the time that the meeting of the cast had broken up. So the caller had known about it. That wasn't all— the caller had seen him come out of Jan's place, had tailed him back to the apartment and then had arranged the deal with Rugger and Marlo. But what did that prove?

Only the cast had known about the meeting. Only the cast and whoever had been told by somebody in the cast. Johnny had waited until the rest of the cast had left before dropping back to Jan's. Which meant . . .

Which meant he was up the creek.

Somebody could have been tailing him all along, could have tailed him to the meeting, waited outside, stayed on his tail while he taxied around the block, then placed the call. If so, Johnny was right back where he had started from. Because such a person did not have to know about the meeting in the first place. He just had to follow Johnny.

He lit another cigarette. The cab stopped in front of his building and he paid off the driver and got out. The doorman looked at him suspiciously, then did a pronounced take and greeted him by name. "Didn't recognize you at first, Mr. Lane," he apologized.

Johnny grinned. The clothes were not exactly his style, he thought. And his nose still had some of the build-up job left on it. No wonder the doorman had missed him the first time around.

The elevator operator did not notice anything different, or if he did he did not say anything one way or the other. He took Johnny up to his penthouse swiftly and silently, and Johnny opened the front door.

He switched on the lights, pretty certain that he had left them on when he had gone out. Which was strange. He thought that Ito might have come home early, then decided that at that particular moment Ito was probably teaching a pretty little girl how to say "Do it again, darling" in English.

Of course, Ito could have dropped in again, and could have turned off the lights on the way out. Or maybe he himself had turned them off and his mind was turned inside-out, or then again maybe . . .

He could not get rid of the nagging suspicion that he wasn't alone in the apartment.

He stopped in front of a mirror to remove the remaining makeup from his face and to unputty his nose. He took off his hat and coat, removed the gun from his shoulder holster. He felt ridiculous—it is remarkably easy to feel silly when you are toting a gun in your own apartment.

Still . . .

He checked each room in the apartment with gun drawn. He looked into the kitchen, opened closet doors, and felt increasingly like an idiot as he inspected each empty room. He even looked into Ito's room, something he never did, and was careful to shut the door when he left. Only his own bedroom remained, and he stood in front of the closed door for several seconds, unable to end the search by opening the damned door.

You're a horse's ass, he told himself angrily. Either you open the silly door or you put the gun away and have a drink.

He felt like knocking.

But he did not knock. He shrugged, annoyed as all hell with himself and he turned the knob and gave the door a shove. The room was dark, naturally enough. He reached for the light and switched it on.

For a moment he felt as though he were a character in somebody's nightmare, probably his own. He blinked his eyes at the light and stared. His bedcovers were thrown back and there was a girl in his bed.

She was naked.

But history was repeating itself only up to a point. No pool of dark blood had flowed from the girl's neck. No razor had slashed her throat. No killer had killed her. She was, as a matter of fact, very much alive.

She propped herself up on her elbows and grinned at him. Her hair fell over her shoulders loosely and sexily. Her eyes were disarmingly lustful.

"A gun yet," Jan Vernon said. "Come on in, Johnny. Make yourself at home. Take off your shoes and loosen your tie and relax. It's about time." She yawned and stretched, magnificently. "About time," she repeated. "I thought you'd never get here."

It was a while before they got around to talking. By the time the initial shock had worn off something altogether different from shock had taken its place. He began by taking off his jacket, and then he removed the rest of his clothing as well.

Then he got into something more comfortable. Jan.

Later he told her about the evening. It was good to have someone to talk with, someone you could let it all out to. And she was an excellent listener.

"You should have stayed with acting," she told him

finally. "That must have been quite a performance. I wish I could have watched you."

He laughed. "I don't know how good I was, really. I wouldn't have won any awards."

"But you pleased the critics, Johnny. And they sound as though they know their business."

"They were easily intimidated," he told her. "One look at me and they were ready to roll over and play dead. I looked like Death walking. They were afraid of me on sight." He sighed. "Now, it could have been different. I could have come on stage . . . same way, but before a big man in the rackets, a guy who wouldn't be scared to look at me. That would have been more of a test."

"You still should get an Oscar. For makeup."

"You should get one yourself," he said, "For—"

"Never mind what for. Did you get anywhere tonight, Johnny? Did you find out anything?"

"Nothing too helpful," he admitted. "I found out who beat me up. I got even with him by knocking him around a little." He shook his head. "Sounds pretty childish, doesn't it?"

"Childish or manly."

"Which?"

"Sometimes they're about the same thing," she said thoughtfully. "But you aren't any further than before?"

"I suppose not."

She sighed. "That's what I tried to tell you," she said. "That you were wasting your time. Let the police handle it, Johnny. Look how far you stuck your neck out. Suppose the fight with Rugger had gone the other way. He would have killed you."

"There wasn't anything to worry about."

She arched her eyebrows. "The hell there wasn't," she said. "There was plenty to worry about. You were sticking your neck way out for nothing."

"You're exaggerating, Jan. I'm in greater danger here in bed with you."

"What's that supposed to mean?"

"Only that you're a little too exuberant," he told her, grinning. "My ribs hurt. You should be a little more restrained."

She laughed easily. "Sorry," she said. "I get carried away. And it's your fault anyway. You loosen the bonds of restraint, Johnny. That's not very nice of you."

They slipped into an easy silence. He lit two cigarettes and gave one of them to her. He smoked and watched the smoke trail lazily to the ceiling.

"Hey," he said.

"Hey what?"

"I was just thinking. How the hell did you get in here tonight?"

She looked at him.

"I know I locked the door," he said. "I wasn't too sure about the lights, but I know damn well I locked the door. Wasn't it locked when you got here? And how did you get past the doorman?"

She fluffed her hair. "A beautiful woman has no problem getting past doormen," she informed him. "I think he thought I was a call girl you had ordered sent up. I smiled at him and went up in the elevator. And the elevator operator never said a word."

"He never does. How about the door?"

She pursed her lips. "Actually," she said, "I thought you'd be home. I would have told you I was coming except I thought I could surprise you."

"You surprised me, all right. But how the hell did you get past the door?"

"I was getting around to that, Johnny. I rang the bell. Several times. You didn't answer."

"Primarily because I wasn't here."

She ignored the interruption. "I didn't want to go home," she said. "And I thought maybe you were drunk or asleep or something and I could get into bed with you and surprise you."

"That would have surprised me, all right. It would have surprised the hell out of me."

"That's what I thought. So I opened the door."

"But it was locked!"

"Not very well," she said, "because I opened it. You ought to lock that door with a key, Johnny. When you just close it, all you have is a spring lock. They're easy to pick."

"You—you picked the lock?"

She nodded, beaming. "With a nail file," she said. "All you have to do is sort of pry at it for a while. A nail file works perfectly. A woman can do almost anything with a bobby pin or a nail file or a . . ."

Then she blushed.

"Almost anything," he said thoughtfully.

"Johnny—"

"But not quite everything. For some things you can't quite get along with a bobby pin or a file. So—"

"Johnny, stop that!"

"Don't be ridiculous," he told her. "You don't want me to stop it. Besides, I've hardly even started."

And he reached for her again.

When he awoke it was morning and she was gone. The telephone on the bedside table was ringing industriously and unpleasantly. He reached for it, then stopped to glance at a note she had left.

"You snore," it read, "but I love you anyway."

He grinned, crumpled the note into a ball and tossed it at a wastebasket. The phone was still ringing and there seemed to be only one way to stop it. He picked it up and said hello into the mouthpiece.

"Pete Galton," a voice said. "New York *Post*—"

"We don't want any," he said.

"Lane—"

"The show's off for this season. No, I don't know who the killer is. No, I don't have a statement to make. Yes, damn you, I was sleeping. Goodbye."

"All I want to know is—"

"To be fully informed," Johnny cooed, "read the *New York Times*."

He put the receiver back long enough to break the

connection, then decided to leave it off the hook. He left it off long enough to hear the dial tone change to that annoying squeal which indicates that your phone is off base, then he gave up and cradled it properly. At which point there was a discreet knock on the door.

"Come in."

The door opened. Ito—a wonderful, marvelous Ito—appeared. He was pushing a small breakfast table on rollers. The tray carried a glass of orange juice, a plate of scrambled eggs and bacon, and a huge mug of black coffee.

"Breakfast in bed," Ito said. "Sorry I couldn't cut off that last phone call. I was busy pouring coffee."

"There been many other calls?"

"Just newspapers. I told them the show was off and you had no statement to make."

Johnny finished the orange juice and picked up a fork. "You took the words right out of my mouth," he said. "That's what I told the gentleman from the *Post*."

Ito left and Johnny went to work on breakfast, which disappeared rapidly. He carried the coffee out to the living room and sat down.

"How was last night?" he asked.

Ito spread out his hands. "So-so."

"Is it true what they say about Japanese women?"

"I'd be the last to know," Ito said. "Is it true what they say about Miss Vernon?"

Johnny gaped.

"She was coming out," Ito explained, "just as I was coming in. Evidently she and I keep equally late hours. Her self-possession was magnificent. She asked me if the weather was still lousy and I assured her that it was, this being New York. Which made her laugh, for some inscrutable reason. Or is inscrutable an adjective to be applied only to Orientals?"

Johnny chuckled. "By the way," he said, "how come the breakfast-in-bed-routine?"

"Because I am grateful for the night out." Ito smiled reminiscently. "A sweet girl. We spoke alternately in English and in Japanese. And do you know what she told me?"

"What?"

"It seems I speak Japanese with a deplorable American accent," Ito said. "Isn't that something?" He frowned. "I've got to stop dating Japanese girls. They're good company. But they all look alike to me."

The day was routine. There was a call from Haig saying that nothing had come up, that they were running down leads and running out of them, that the wheels of police procedure were grinding away like the mills of the gods. Johnny wanted to continue the metaphor to a logical conclusion by pointing out that they were grinding exceedingly small, but he did not have the heart. Haig told him to mind his own business—gently—and to let the police take care of things. Johnny explained that he had no intention of interfering with police work, put the receiver down and took his tongue out of his cheek.

The rest of the day he devoted to paperwork.

Correspondence—some of it vital and the bulk of it trivial—had piled up during the past several days. Johnny sat at his desk in his study and paid bills, wrote letters, canceled arrangements and scrawled memos.

Time passed.

It was two-thirty in the afternoon when Ito knocked softly on the door. Johnny let him into the study.

"I didn't mean to bother you," Ito said. "There's a . . . a young man here. He wants to see you. I don't think you want to see him."

"Why?"

"I think he's insane," Ito confided. "He seems to have a monumental aversion to soap and water. Perhaps it's an allergy."

Johnny grinned.

"And his dialogue is unusual," Ito said. "He told me I was probably a . . . a groove at clapping one hand. Whatever that means. His name is—"

"Lennie Schwerner," Johnny said. "He's not crazy exactly. He's a Zen Buddhist."

Johnny strode past the startled Ito. "Don't look so alarmed," he said. "Your country doesn't have a monopoly on Zen Buddhists anymore. I guess I'd better see him."

Chapter Twelve

Lennie Schwerner was in the living room. He was sitting in Johnny's chair and smoking one of Johnny's cigarettes. His pose indicated that he was imagining the penthouse was his own, and that the prospect pleased him.

"You shook up Ito a little," Johnny told him. "What's the bit about clapping one hand?"

"A *koan*," Schwerner explained.

"Like an ice cream cone? I—"

The kid spelled the word. "A Zen question. You know, like I saw him coming on so Japanese-like and I figure it's his country so I'll hit him with a *koan*." He paused. "I don't think he was impressed."

"He was just being inscrutable," Johnny assured him. "Ito was impressed. How does the *koan* go?"

"We all know the sound of two hands clapping. But what is the sound of one hand clapping?"

Johnny nodded. "Uh-huh. Semantic, sort of. There an answer to go with the question?"

"There are a few," Schwerner said. "The one I like best says the sound is that silence created by the absence of the second hand." He paused. "It's to find new ways of looking at things, I guess. It sharpens your mind."

"Might make a good title," Johnny mused. "*Clap One Hand.* Something like that." He shrugged. "You wanted to see me," he said. "What's on your mind? Outside of one-handed applause, that is."

Lennie put out his cigarette. "I read about this other murder," he said. His voice sounded younger now. "That actor, Carter Tracy. I saw him in a lot of pictures. When I was a kid I used to groove the war movies—you know, where he was the colonel and they were having dogfights with MIG's around the Yalu River and he was in love with this married broad."

"I must have missed it."

"I saw it seven times," Lennie said. "Each time it had a different title and a different actress playing the married broad. But it was always good old Carter Tracy as the colonel. Or captain, or major, or something. And now he's dead."

Johnny nodded. The kid had something to say and Johnny wondered when he would get around to saying it. Johnny could not afford to listen to old movie plots all day long. At the same time, he did not want to rush Schwerner. He waited.

"Groovy pad you got here. Must cost you heavy bread, huh?"

"It's not cheap."

"Yeah," Lennie said. "Penthouse on Fifth Avenue with a view of the park. You got a terrace, too?"

"A balcony."

The boy nodded. "Yeah. You know what I pay where I live? Thirty-seven bucks a month. That's with electricity tossed in. It's unheated, of course. I picked up a pair of gas heaters for three-and-a-half bucks apiece and hooked 'em up."

He put out his cigarette. "I think Elaine was paying more," he said. "Her pad was a little larger. I think she said she was shelling out forty, maybe forty-five. And she had more stairs to climb. But you saw her place, didn't you?"

Johnny nodded. "I saw it."

"And she was going to move uptown. She didn't talk much but she dropped a word here, a phrase there. Talking about something on a high floor by the East River. Paying forty-five tops a month and talking about the East River. When you can't pay more dough than that you don't go looking at the East River. You jump in it."

Johnny offered him another cigarette. He took it and accepted a light. He dragged hard on the cigarette and blew out smoke. He took another drag and let it out slowly.

"I don't know why I came here," Lennie said suddenly. "I had a few ideas after you cut out yesterday. Ideas about why Elaine caught it. I was going to talk to you, fill you in. Then I read about this Tracy and how he caught it the same way. It switched things around, you know?"

"I know."

"I thought Elaine got killed for a reason. You know, like she was taking chances shaking down some cat and he got rid of her. That's ugly all by itself. But at least it adds up that way. You can say all right, she was a nice chick and all, but she was kind of a bitch and she got killed for a reason. That way it makes a little sense. It's still ugly but it makes sense. But this way! Man, she was killed because she was there. She was in your show and somebody was down on your show and she caught it in the neck." Lennie paused, shaking his head. "Bad," he said. "It's bad to get killed at all. It's worse to get killed for no reason. It can't get much worse than that."

Johnny looked at him. "You could use a drink, Lennie."

"That's an idea."

He got a bottle and poured short ones, tossing one down his throat and handing the other to the kid. Lennie sipped the bourbon slowly, appreciatively. He put the shot glass down empty.

"Thanks," he said. "I suppose I should get the hell home. Sit on the floor and contemplate the perfection of the universe and the *karma* of all things. I'm wasting your time."

"You came here to tell me something, didn't you?"

"I thought so. I'm not sure now. You know why I fell up here? Because it hurts to sit still. Somebody killed a girl I knew. I wasn't in love with her, I wasn't sleeping with her—I just knew her and liked her a little. So it's rough to sit around contemplating the perfection of the universe while the bastard who killed her walks around free."

Johnny knew what he meant. He felt the same way himself. But there was not a hell of a lot else to do. He had tried last night, and after a bucketful of clever acting and a barrelful of theatrical gymnastics, all he had managed to do was beat the hell out of a muscle-bound oaf with his brains in his fists. Johnny had not found out a thing that helped him. He had not narrowed down the range of suspects; more accurately, he hadn't turned up a single suspect.

"I thought of something," Lennie went on. "Only I guess it doesn't make it any more. It's like *passé*."

"And you were bringing it to me?"

The boy nodded.

"Why not to the cops?"

"The fuzz don't dig me too much. They look at me and all they see is the beard."

"Some aren't too bad," Johnny said, thinking of Haig. "Some of them—"

"To hell with them," Lennie said. "About Elaine. I got to meditating, sort of, and I came up with a notion. I thought of somebody who might have killed her. But that was before Tracy got hit. That changed things."

"Who were you thinking of?"

Lennie shrugged. "Doesn't matter. I was buggy coming here in the first place. I guess I just had eyes to talk to somebody and you were handy. Thanks for listening."

He got to his feet and started for the door.

"Hold it—"

The boy stopped, turned around. "Yeah?"

"You got this far," Johnny told him. "You wasted this much time. So you might as well waste a minute or two more. You said you thought you knew who killed Elaine—"

"That's history now."

"So make like a historian."

"What good's it gonna do?"

Johnny took a deep breath. The kid was right—what good was it going to do? But in a mess like this anything could help. The only thing to do was gather every scrap of information that happened to crop up.

"Tell me about it," Johnny said steadily. "Sit down, relax, and tell me about it. Want another drink?"

"I better not."

"Then just talk."

Lennie said, "It's nothing, really. Just a guy she talked about."

"What's his name?"

"She didn't mention it. Or if she did I don't remember. I got a rotten memory for names."

"He was in the cast?"

"Yeah. I don't know what he did. She told me but I forget. He had this big yen for her. According to her, he spent a lot of time bugging her. Coaching her in her part, then making silly passes at her. Nutty ones. You know, like falling down in front of her and kissing her feet. Bugged, you dig?"

"Go on."

"That's it. He would switch back and forth all the time. One minute the bit is she's the greatest actress since Duse and the world's going to love her. The next minute she's no damn good at all. He was coming on hot and cold like that and she didn't know where she stood with him. That got her all shook up." He paused significantly. "That was very important to her," he told Johnny. "The theater, I mean.

Her career. She was sincere as all hell about it. She may have been a cheap little bitch in a lot of ways but she was straight on the acting scene. It was important to her, man."

"I know that."

"She really cared. She wanted to be an actress in a big way. I don't know how good she was—"

"Really good," Johnny said.

"And she never got the chance." Lennie Schwerner stared hard at the floor. His hand went to his beard—a scrawny, unkempt beard that somehow did not look nearly so ridiculous to Johnny anymore. The boy stroked the beard idly. "Back to this cat," he said finally. "He was bugging her, especially when he would do his switch and scream on her, telling her she couldn't act her way out of a cardboard box. But she didn't mind that after a while. Because he was the same way about the show itself, she told me. One minute it was the greatest thing since *King Lear* and it would sail through two thousand performances. The next minute it was lousy. It was the worst script in the world. It shouldn't be produced. It would be a crime to have the play produced and—"

He stopped when he saw the expression on Johnny's face.

"I said something?"

"Maybe."

"What's the pitch?"

"To hell with the pitch," Johnny snapped. "First, let's figure out who the man is."

Lennie looked at him. "I said something important?"

"Yeah. And for the wrong reason. I don't want to go into it now. But somebody connected with the show—hell, it could be anybody. A stage manager, an assistant prop hand, anybody in the damned business. She was ready to listen to anybody when it came to acting. I gave her a few hours of instruction myself."

He stopped suddenly and swallowed. "Hell," he said, "this mystery man couldn't be me, could it? I get depressed about shows. I bawl people out. I—"

"You ever kiss her feet?"

"What the—"

"Then that lets you out," Schwerner said patiently. "This cat kissed her feet. So—"

"Anybody. Anybody from the set designer to the third assistant pencil sharpener to the costume director to the—"

"Director!"

Johnny stared. Schwerner was snapping his fingers, his eyes alert now. "That was it," he said. "Some kind of a director. What's the director's name?"

"Ernie Buell. But—"

"Buell. Ernie Buell. Ernie, Ernest. Buell."

"It ring a bell?"

"A whole steepleful," the boy said. "That's the foot-kisser. That's our boy."

Buell was married, Johnny thought. Buell was a happily married guy with a pair of kids. Buell—

Buell was also a little bit nuts.

"What do we do now, man? What do we do?"

Johnny looked at the boy. "Sit down," he said. "Sit down and I'll tell you."

It was amazing how neatly the pieces fitted when you saw the way to put them together. It was absolutely incredible how obvious everything became once it was obvious.

Johnny ground out a cigarette in an ashtray. He listened to Lennie Schwerner talk quietly on the telephone. He followed the conversation until the boy grinned hugely and hung up.

"It's set," Lennie said.

"He fell for it?"

"He fell on his face. I gave him the pitch straight from the armpit and he ate it up. I'm a blackmailer. Elaine told me all about him and I can prove he killed Elaine and Tracy. But I'm not the talkative type. I can be had for the right price."

"How did he react?"

"Like clockwork. I told him to meet me at Topp's on Forty-second Street. You must have heard that."

"Yeah. He's meeting you?"

"In fifteen minutes, he says. He can't do anything in a crowded restaurant, can he?"

"He's not that cracked. But I'll go along with you, anyway. Just for protection."

Lennie shook his head violently. "He'd spot you," he said. "And that would tear it."

"But—"

"Please." The boy's tone was suddenly quite firm. Johnny let him talk. "Don't you see, man? I got to do this by myself. I got to go down and meet this cat and pull everything out of him, and then I can hand him to you and you can hand him to the fuzz or whatever you want to do with him. But I gotta set it up on my own. It has to be my scene."

"For Elaine?"

Schwerner shook his head. "Not for Elaine. For me. After this I can go back to Yonkers and sell insurance. I can shave twice a day and wear a Brooks Brothers suit and join the Kiwanis. I can marry a bridge-playing chick and contribute to the population explosion. But first I have to do something that means something. Something real." He lowered his eyes. "Okay, so I'm coming on too strong. But it's a moment-of-truth type of scene. I'm the matador and the bull is coming at me and all I've got in my hand is this short sword. I can't cop out now. I can't grab a gun and shoot the bull. I have to use the sword, and by myself."

Johnny understood.

"I'll be safe in there. I'll be ice-cool, stoned on my own nerve endings. Don't worry."

After Lennie Schwerner left, Johnny sat and smoked and tried to see how he had missed knowing all along that the killer was Buell. Everything pointed that way now. Everything.

The buggy aspect figured. The two bodies, both so nude and so dead, one a man and the other a girl. Buell had been in and out of loony bins for a long time. Nobody had ever accused him of being sane.

Evidently he was a hell of a lot sicker than anybody had ever realized. Sick enough to lose touch with reality.

Sick enough to kill.

From there on it was easy. Buell alternately loved and hated the show, just as he loved and hated everybody he knew, according to his mood. He had made a passionate speech defending the play at the cast meeting, but in preliminary rehearsals he had frequently run the script into the ground. He had thought Elaine was wonderful, marvelous, perfect. But there were times when he had screamed at her hysterically.

Johnny had tried to ignore this, chalking it up to artistic temperament. There was a thin line between genius and insanity, sometimes no line at all. The areas had an annoying tendency to overlap.

They had overlapped, in Buell.

The director loved the script. But at the same time he hated it—maybe because he was scared of it, terrified that he could not give it the direction it deserved. In public he praised and defended the show. In private he tried to sink it.

That, Johnny guessed, was a part of the reason for Elaine's murder. Although Buell's motive went a little further. Elaine was good, perfect—with her gone the show would be a shadow. But Elaine was not entirely perfect. No one is, on-stage or off. So in one sense Buell could see her as ruining the script by being less than perfect.

And then there was the sex angle. The foot-kissing

routine, coupled with his periodic disdain for her and her perpetual unwillingness to lose her virginity.

It added up.

And, the beating. That figured, too. Buell had gone to the cast meeting against his will. Once there, he had done his damnedest to save the show, hold the cast together. Then the meeting had ended and he had done the Jekyll-and-Hyde bit. The plan he had set up with Rugger and Marlo earlier in the day went into play.

That whole episode had had the touch of an accomplished director, Johnny reflected. The method of contact with the two thugs, set up so that they could not identify him because they did not so much as see him or hear his natural voice. He had used kids for messengers, had even made a single hundred-dollar bill do the work of two and thus had removed any possibility of identification during a final payoff.

Then, when the meeting had broken up, he had stayed on Johnny's tail. He was biding his time, taking it easy. If Johnny had gone straight home, Buell would have let the thing ride for a day. He did not have to worry about time. But Johnny had returned to Jan's. And that was the set-up. A couple of quick calls to Rugger and Marlo, and Buell was on his way home with Johnny targeted like a clay pigeon.

It was pretty, you had to give Buell that.

Carter Tracy's murder had been a little different. It was not hard to spot a few reasons for Tracy's death. First of all, the show was still supposed to go on. The death of the female lead had not been enough to stop it. The male lead also had to go.

There was more, just as there had been more with Elaine. Tracy must have been a monumental thorn in Ernie Buell's side. The actor's ego had been insufferable. His success with women had been legendary. And that ability with women could only have irritated Ernie, who was awkward with the opposite sex and ugly as sin— and who had not gotten with Elaine. Tracy had probably boasted to Ernie that he was sleeping with the girl. The actor had belonged to the lay-and-tell school, Johnny knew. He had leered boastfully while informing Johnny that he knew where Jan's apartment was, that he had been there before. He could have leered the same way when discussing Elaine, without any real justification.

So Buell had killed him.

Johnny lit one cigarette from the butt of another, and waited.

The phone rang.

Johnny snatched it up. He said hello and waited for Lennie Schwerner's voice. But the voice that answered was not that of the bearded boy. It was Haig's.

"A little complication," Sam Haig said apologetically. "Sorry to bother you. This is probably just a waste of time, but I had to check it out with you."

Johnny held his breath. Everybody was apologizing to

him, he thought. Everybody was worried about wasting his time. What was so damned important about his time?

"Got a call from your director," Haig went on. "Ernest Buell. He said some nut called him on the phone and threatened to blackmail him for killing Tracy and the James girl. He arranged a meeting with the nut and called us. We went down to Topp's on Times Square and picked the nut up. He's nuts, all right. A beatnik. He's got a beard looks like hell."

Johnny's brain was whirring in circles. He felt as if his head were going to come off.

Haig was talking again.

"So I had to bother you," he said. "This nut, his name is Leonard Schwerner. He came up with this story that he's a friend of yours. That you know him. That you sent him with a phony story for Buell, for your own reasons. We have to follow up everything. You know that. So I called."

Johnny closed his eyes. He had found, over the years, that some blows were easier to take with your eyes closed. Often, when things got rough, you could make them less so by closing your eyes. It sometimes helped.

This time it did not.

"You still there, Johnny?"

"Yeah," he said hollowly. "I guess so."

"You don't happen to know this Schwerner character, do you? I feel like an idiot asking, but—"

"I know him."

"No kidding. I thought he was completely nuts. But this story of his is garbage, right?"

"Wrong." Johnny took a deep breath. He swallowed. "Lennie Schwerner is telling the truth," he managed to force out. "I sent him to Buell. I arranged the whole thing, Sam. The kid is not nuts."

There was an extraordinarily long pause.

"You get yourself down here," Haig said.

"Where?"

"My office," Haig said. "I got Buell here and I got Schwerner here and I want you here. Fast."

Chapter Thirteen

It could have been comic.

High comedy, say. Or low comedy. Whichever way you played it, it had all the ingredients of a thoroughly hysterical scene. The famous director Ernest Buell, furious as a cuckolded husband in a French bedroom farce. Lennie Schwerner, bearded and bedraggled, trembling like the would-be beggar in *Three-Penny Opera* under the wrath of Peachum. Haig, mad as hell, and Johnny, trying to explain things so that they made sense.

It could have been a riot. All the potentials were there and with the right direction it might have been the funniest event since Charlie Chaplin's debut. There was only one thing wrong.

Direction was completely lacking.

It went every which way, so it turned out tragic instead of comic.

The curtain rose with Johnny storming into Haig's office at headquarters. Buell was sitting on one side of Haig's desk, glowering. Schwerner sat on Haig's other side and looked very small. An incongruous handcuff shackled him to his chair.

"Hold him," Johnny snapped.

"Don't worry about it," Haig said, tapping Lennie on the shoulder. "He's not going to run very far. He'd have to carry the chair on his back, and . . ."

"Not him, damn it. Buell!"

Haig stared.

"Buell did it," Johnny said. "He killed Elaine and Tracy. He set me up for a mugging. He's not entirely sane, Haig. He's off his rocker. Now, Sam, hear this—"

Johnny explained it all, carefully, patiently, and at length. He went over the entire case, giving in detail everything he had managed to piece together to show that Buell had to be the killer. Johnny filled in the psychological background, told how Buell both hated and loved the play, how he felt the same way about Elaine. By the time he was finished, all three of the men in the room regarded him with something approaching awe.

Buell spoke first.

"That's nice," he said. "You know, I thought you liked me, Lane. Some people hold it against a man that he's spent time in a mental hospital. That never showed in your attitude toward me. I'm glad I've found out how you really feel."

Something was wrong. Buell did not sound like a man who had just been accused of double murder and quadruple insanity. In fact, he seemed calmer now than Johnny had ever known him to be.

"It's not a nice thing to find out," Buell went on conversationally. "I was beginning to enjoy working with you.

You're a good producer. You handle people well. But now I won't ever be able to do a show with you. It's a shame, in a way."

"Look—"

"You look," Buell said. His voice hardened. "You've just given me grounds for seven different kinds of a slander suit. You've defamed my character to hell and back."

"You killed them, Buell. Admit it."

"The hell I will." Buell sighed. "When Elaine was killed I was home all night with my wife. We had guests. Respectable people. They will so testify, Johnny."

"But—"

"When Tracy was killed," the director went on, "I was with my analyst. I've never claimed to be in perfect mental or emotional health, Lane. I'm not. I have my ups and downs, as you know. I go to an analyst regularly. I'm trying to straighten myself out. It's not easy."

Johnny swallowed.

"I've been hot and cold toward the play, of course. I've been moody. But not so moody as you make out." He looked away. "And I must admit to rather strong feelings regarding Elaine James. She could have been a great actress, Lane. I was enthusiastic about her."

"How enthusiastic?"

"I—I kissed her feet, Lane. Yes. Is that what you want me to say? It's one of the few damned things that's saving you from a slander suit, you know. It wouldn't do me any good to have it brought up in a courtroom. I suspect the damned press would have a field day with an item like that.

You can be pretty goddamned glad I kissed her feet, you son of a bitch."

"Ernie—"

"I suppose I loved her. A strange sort of love, I admit. A worshipful love. I wanted to get past that strange reserve of hers. I wanted to reach her. But I didn't kill her, Lane. I did not cut her throat. And you're a rotten bastard to think so."

He stood up and walked out of the room.

Johnny turned his head to watch Buell go, then winced at the sound of the door slamming. He fumbled the pack of cigarettes from his jacket pocket, shook a cigarette free and stuck it into his mouth. He lit it without turning to face Haig. He took a deep drag that seared his throat.

He turned around slowly.

"You're just letting him go?" he croaked. "First you should check him out. He . . . it could all be cleverness, understand. He's very clever. And now he's getting away and—"

"Johnny."

He stopped in mid-sentence.

"Johnny, we checked Buell's alibi. We checked it a long time ago. We checked him out thoroughly the morning after Elaine James was killed. He was completely in the clear on that one, home with some friends all night. We checked him again when Tracy was killed. That second check was purely a matter of form, just routine. We learned he was on a psychiatrist's couch while somebody was giving Tracy the closest and last shave of his life. Buell was at a business appointment before that and home for dinner after that."

"Uh—"

"So he didn't do anything," Haig said. "He was complete-ly clear. You came up with a nice fresh suspect. One that us dumb cops never would have thought up. You worked up a pretty little theory and you played it to the hilt. That was real smart, Johnny. It was a bright thing to do."

"Hold on, Sam. You heard how it went together. All right—it was wrong. But at the time—"

"It looked good?"

"Damn good."

Haig heaved a sigh. "That's great," he said. "That's dandy. I'm not knocking your theory, Johnny. You and Bristle Face worked it up nice. It made sense."

"Then—"

"Then you should have called me," the cop said. "Jesus, suppose you were right. You think we couldn't have gotten more out of Buell in a grill room than this kid here could get over a beer or two at Topp's?" He turned on Lennie. "You're a real smart kid," he said. "You thought this Buell character was a lunatic. So you were going to sit down and play checkers with him. That was pretty clever. Suppose he took out a gun and shot a hole in your head? Where would you be then?"

Lennie's face fell. "He wouldn't have come on like that," the boy said. But his tone was uncertain.

"Of course not," Haig said. "He would do what any in-telligent person would do. That's what he did. He called me first. Then he went down to Topp's with us behind him.

And then we picked you up, you damn fool and now you're chained to your chair like a monkey."

Lennie hung his head. Johnny felt monumentally sorry for him at that particular moment. And it wasn't the kid's fault. Johnny was to blame—he had to indulge his flair for the theatrical approach instead of using his fat head. And because of that, because of him, Schwerner was in trouble.

"You know what I could do with you, kid?" Sam Haig was rubbing it in. "Buell's slander suit would be only the beginning. Attempted extortion would go on top of that. For that you go to prison. I've got half a mind to toss you in the Tombs overnight to cool off. Might put some sense in your head. It—"

"Leave him alone, Sam."

Haig turned. "You've got something to say?"

"Just leave him alone," Johnny blurted. "None of this mess is Lennie's fault. All he did was come to me with some information. I took the ball and ran with it. I got him to phone Ernie and set up the meeting. So don't blame him, Sam. He was just following my instructions."

"Then you weren't very bright, Johnny." Haig's voice was relentless. "You could have called me. I'd have told you Buell was clean and that would have been that. Or I'd have run a check on him again for the hell of it, just to make sure. Instead, you took your act on the road and got stranded. You didn't do it right, Johnny."

"I know."

"I don't try and tell you how to run your plays, Johnny.

I don't pick your cast or read over your script or get in your way. I wait until your show opens, and then I buy a pair of tickets—"

"When did you last buy a ticket?"

Haig sighed. "I take the tickets you send me," he amended, "and I see the show. That's all. Why are you trying to handle my job for me, Johnny?"

"I don't know."

"No reason at all?"

"It's just the way my mind works," Johnny said honestly. "I hardly even considered calling you. I just looked for a way to trap Ernie, to catch him."

Haig glared for several seconds. "I ought to jail both of you," he said. "But the hell with it. The city's too busy rehabilitating drunks and tapering off junkies. I can't be bothered."

He picked up a key from his desk, leaned over and unlocked Lennie's handcuffs.

"You know," he told Johnny, "I'd like to take this kid and hang a murder rap on him. But no jury in the world would listen twice."

Haig looked, suddenly, as though he were going to start laughing. "You could pin anything on a bum like this one," he said almost affectionately. "Anything from arson to sodomy. Anything but this particular murder. You know why?"

Johnny asked why.

"Because he doesn't own a razor," Haig said. "Ain't that a hell of a note?"

* * *

Everything, Johnny thought, was getting to be a hell of a note. Anything and everything.

He loaded Lennie Schwerner into a cab, although the kid insisted that the subway would be fine. Johnny gave the driver a buck and told him to take the kid home.

"I'm sorry," Lennie said for perhaps the thousandth time. "Like I blew it."

"You did all right," Johnny assured him. "I was the one who blew it. And don't let what Haig said get you down. You're okay. I think he likes you."

"He digs me like the plague."

Johnny took a breath. "When you give up the Zen kick," he said, "why don't you give me a ring?"

"What for?"

"Because you don't sound too enthusiastic about insurance. You might like the theater business."

"Yeah, sure. I'll be an actor."

"There are other sides to show business. There's the whole production end. A smart kid can find a place for himself. And talent has nothing to do with it."

"You serious?"

Johnny nodded. "Go think about it," he said. "Go home, get in a full lotus posture and meditate. Clap one hand or something. In a week or so give me a ring and let me know if you're interested. I might be able to find you something."

"You're serious," Schwerner said, his voice strangely airy. "You're actually serious."

"Uh-huh."

"But—"

"Go think about it. I'll see you."

He turned and sidled away from the cab, watched it pull off with the boy still turned around in his seat, staring back at Johnny. He waited on the curb until the cab was around the corner, then pitched the cigarette he had been smoking into the gutter and stepped out to snare a cab for himself. The first half-dozen had fares. Then an empty stopped for him and he got into the back seat and gave the cabby his address.

If they gave awards for stupidity, he thought, he would have one coming. Or maybe a dozen.

He thought about Ernie Buell, accused of two killings. Johnny had managed to lose the services of one of the best directors on Broadway, to lose the man permanently. Ernest Buell would never work for Johnny again—for which Johnny could hardly blame the man. In all probability Ernie would never even speak to him again, and he couldn't blame Ernie for that either.

And the theory had seemed so perfect . . .

Proving, Johnny decided, that things were seldom as they seemed. He stared glumly through the cab window at the night. Night? Sure, night already—and how exactly had that happened? He wasn't sure. It seemed to him as though time lately had discovered a way of going slowly one moment and then speeding up. How many days since he had found Elaine's body? He couldn't even remember.

Night. Dull gray night, with the tourists from Omaha and Cripple Creek hurrying to see the right shows and dine at the right restaurants and, if they were here on business and their wives were home in Omaha or Cripple Creek, to sleep with the right call girls. Night, when the city came to life. Or to death.

The cab stopped. Johnny tipped the driver, nodded blankly at the doorman, ignored the elevator operator as thoroughly as the latter ignored him. He did not have the strength to hunt for his key. He rang the bell and Ito opened the door.

"Well," Ito said brightly. "How did it go?"

It was the wrong thing to say. Johnny's shoulders slumped. He walked past the servant without a word, found the easy chair in the living room and sank into it with a groan. Ito apparently recognized the dimensions of his error; he was on hand quickly with a glass of bourbon, which soon was empty.

"In answer to your ill-advised question," Johnny said finally, "it went horribly."

Ito knew better than to say anything more. He turned and padded away.

"Ito—"

He came back.

"Sit down for a minute. Let me give you the score. It makes a good story."

He told Ito, which helped somewhat. He told him, and while telling him he remembered the British maxim that no man is a hero to his valet, and he decided that that no man was a hero to his butler, either. Especially when you let the butler know just how much of a hero you weren't.

He finished. And Ito, eyes sympathetic and voice well modulated, said: "I see."

"Is that all you can say?"

"There is ancient proverb," Ito said. "Man who put both feet in mouth not need kick in teeth."

"You're a sweetheart," Johnny said. "Where the hell do you get those Japanese proverbs?"

"It's a fake Chinese proverb," Ito said. "I stole it from Charlie Chan. So the whole thing is back where it was at the beginning, right?"

"Which means nowhere."

Ito nodded. "There's one aspect that intrigues me," he said. "Both the girl and the man were found nude in bed. They were both nude when they were killed."

"Not necessarily."

"No?"

"The killer could have stripped them after they were dead."

Ito thought it over. "There were no bloody clothes around," he said. "And there was blood on their bodies. This seems somehow significant. At least to the Oriental mind."

Johnny stared at him.

"They were killed nude," Ito said. "True?" Johnny closed his eyes. He remembered Elaine James, saw once more the blood that had flowed into the valley between her young breasts. He saw Carter Tracy, with blood matting the hairs on his chest.

Johnny nodded slowly. "I guess so."

"If both were killed nude," Ito said, "and if both were killed by the same person—"

"Yeah," Johnny said. "Yeah, I see what you're getting at. But it doesn't add up. It—"

He broke off suddenly and stood up. He plunged both hands into his pockets and began to pace the floor, covering the living room in long firm strides, his mind buzzing.

Patterns were emerging.

"It couldn't be," he said softly. "It couldn't be. It's too far-fetched. It's impossible."

Ito wisely said nothing.

Johnny grabbed a cigarette, snapped a match into flame. He crossed the room again, this time to the door that led to the balcony. He opened the door and stepped out to the small balcony. He looked down at the traffic on Fifth Avenue, gazed across at the park. He leaned against the railing and smoked the cigarette until only a small butt was left. He stepped on the butt and went inside again, closing the balcony door behind him. The telephone directory was on the lower shelf of the table where the phone itself rested. He picked up the book, thumbed through it quickly, and cursed.

Lennie Schwerner was not listed. Well, Johnny thought, it almost figured. When you lived in a hole in the wall and paid thirty-five bucks or so a month for rent, you didn't have a phone. On the other hand, if your father was in the insurance business . . .

On a hunch he dialed Information. And, happily, Lennie

Schwerner did have a phone, a new listing. Johnny dialed the number and the boy answered on the second ring.

"Johnny Lane, here. I've got a question for you."

"About a job? I been thinking, man. And—"

"Forget that for now. This is more important."

"Lay it on me," Lennie said.

And Johnny fired his question.

"Yeah," Lenny said. "Yeah, that's the way it was. I suppose I should have told you before."

"Why the hell didn't you?"

Johnny could picture the boy shrugging his shoulders. "*De mortuis*," Lennie said. "And I didn't think it was important. Why scream on a corpse? *De mortuis* and *de gustibus*. It was her scene."

Johnny thanked him and hung up. That filled everything in, he thought. That tied all the knots neatly.

Too neatly?

Now, he supposed, he should go to Haig and lay the whole thing in his lap. But that would not work, damn it! It was not that he was trying to play policeman, not at all. But, Haig would never be able to get anywhere with this one, not now. Johnny had to handle this one by himself.

If it blew up in his face, too bad. But this would not be another Ernie Buell fiasco. It couldn't be. And Johnny would handle it smoothly, easily, with the softest of kid gloves. If by some chance he turned out wrong, the world would not fall in. He would be covered, if he played it right.

He did not want to be right, though. He hoped he would be proved wrong.

"I've got another bright idea," he told Ito. "I'm going to think about it for a few minutes. Think it over under a hot shower. If anybody calls, I'm not home."

"Not to anyone?"

"Not to anyone," Johnny said firmly. He went to his bedroom, undressed, then ran the shower and stepped tinder it. It was too hot, which was fine with him. He let the jet of water blast into the back of his neck. His muscles relaxed. His bandages—the ones that were supposed to be holding his chest together—got wet. He had forgotten them during all that concentrated thought. Which proved that thinking was dangerous, probably. Which was something he had been discovering all night long.

He grabbed a cake of soap and worked up a lather. Suppose he took his ideas to Haig? What would the cop do? Tell him to go chase himself, probably. Or try to run down the theory and run, instead, into a stone wall. So he had to play it all by himself; he had to make a Lane Production out of it.

Would it work?

Mentally, he ran through it—not like a cop but like a producer and writer and director rolled into one. He saw it all in terms of lines of dialogue and tricks of lighting and subtle stage directions. He let the blocking work itself out, and by the time he stepped out of the shower the entire show had taken form in his mind.

It would work.

In the matter of Ernie Buell, Johnny had allowed himself to be carried away. The set-up had been too perfect and so

Johnny had allowed himself to be convinced that it could not miss. So he had sent Lennie after Buell with a straightforward and rather meaningless accusation that had backfired horribly. But this time Johnny would be protected.

The pitch would be a curve, breaking away from the outside corner of the theatrical plate. If the batter were innocent it would go wide for a ball. If the batter were guilty there would be a swing and a miss and the ball game would be over.

He had managed to inject a baseball metaphor into a theatrical approach to crime, he thought. Which was ridiculous. But at least he knew what he meant.

He dried himself, noting that most of his bandages had come off—the shower had finished the job his perspiration had started. To hell with it, he thought. He tore off the remaining bandages, dressed quickly but carefully, selecting a television-blue shirt with a spread collar and a wool challis tie with a navy-blue background. He put on a blue blazer with gleaming brass buttons and a pair of light gray slacks. He inspected himself in the mirror and grinned wryly.

Dashing, he told himself. Magnificent.

Ito told him that nobody had called, and handed him another small shot of bourbon which quickly joined the others. Johnny grabbed a hat and a coat, told Ito he'd be back eventually, and left the apartment.

Good old Lennie Schwerner, Johnny thought. Beat, bearded, and bug-headed. A good kid, a bright kid, but a kid who had managed to save the really important information for last. The useless stuff had come to light right away. The one little chunk of information putting everything in a new light had been given a back seat. "I didn't think it was important, man," Lennie had said.

Johnny crossed Fifth Avenue and stepped out from the curb to hail a cab. A bus stopped for him and he waved it away impatiently. The bus opened its doors, hesitated, closed them and drove off into the night. Buses in New York stopped only when you did not want them to, he thought. And he wondered if there were a Zen maxim to cover that. What had Lennie Schwerner called them. *Koans,* he remembered. Anyway, now he was preparing to set up Lennie Schwerner in the production end of the theater business. Make him a third assistant curtain puller or something. Well, the kid had a natural bent for it. A clear-cut sense of the dramatic. Save the punch for the end, and hit 'em hard with it.

Sure.

A cab stopped. Johnny got into it, spoke an address. He pulled the rear door shut behind him and the cab took off. He lit a cigarette.

Two maxims. *De mortuis nil nisi bonum,* meaning speak well of the dead. *De gustibus non disputandum est,* meaning you couldn't argue with matters of taste.

Sure.

Johnny sighed heavily. Those two little scraps of Latin had kept a rather crucial fact hidden in the shrubbery. Elaine James, God rest her soul, had had an abnormal approach to sex. A mystic attitude, Sondra Barr had called it. And then Sonny had broken up in laughter and tears.

Sure.

Mystic? Johnny supposed that was a word for it, if not a particularly good word. There was a better word for it.

Elaine James had been not mystic, but lesbian.

Chapter Fourteen

The meter read ninety-five cents. He took a single from his wallet and looked through his pockets for change.

There was none. He found another single in his wallet, gave them both to the driver, and received a puzzled stare in return. "It's only ninety-five," the driver said. "What's with two bucks?"

Johnny took one back.

"Only a nickel tip?"

Johnny closed his eyes for a moment, then returned the second bill to the driver. "Give half of it to the Red Cross," he said.

The man was stunned. Johnny told him pleasantly to go to hell and watched him drive away.

Johnny lit another cigarette. He was smoking too heavily, he decided. Eventually he would have to cut down. But not now. Not just yet.

He stood on the sidewalk for a minute or two, getting his bearings, silently rehearsing his lines. Then he went into the building and climbed a flight of stairs. He stood in front of the door and looked at the gleaming brass knocker on it. He took a deep breath.

He had a part to play, a part to live. It was more than a matter of committing lines to memory. He had to let himself fall into the proper mood, had to slide into the role headfirst. And his audience would be a most exacting one. There would be no warm-up in New Haven or Philly, no dress rehearsal, no opportunity to rework the script if it looked a little ragged around the edges the first time through. Because the first time was the only time there was going to be. It was opening night already, with all the critics on the aisle and not an empty seat in the house.

He looked at his watch. It was wrong, he decided. Because the real time was 8:40. Curtain time. And the show had to go on.

He raised the knocker, banged on the door firmly. He waited, trying hard to be calm as the part demanded that he be, trying to play the role perfectly.

Then Jan Vernon opened the door and the curtain went up.

"Johnny—"

"I wanted to see you," he said. "And I didn't feel like calling first."

"You should have called. I look like hell."

"You look fine to me."

She did look fine, although obviously she had not been expecting company. She was wearing a wrapper and a pair of broken-down house slippers. Her lipstick had mostly worn off and her hair needed combing. But she still exuded sex and a wholesome, fetching attractiveness. He was not sure how she managed it. It was more earthiness than prettiness, he knew. And that wonderful, fiery body giving out its own symbols.

"I look like hell," she told him again. "But how come you're here? Did you find out something?"

"I haven't even been trying," he said.

"Then—"

He pushed the door closed with one hand. Then he reached for her and took her into his arms. She came willingly enough but he sensed a slight stiffening of muscles, a certain amount of tension. Stiffness and tension both disappeared quickly and her mouth met his for a kiss.

He held her close. Her body was warm under the wrapper, her skin smooth. He knew how that skin felt, how warm and fresh it was. He knew that body. He had made love to it twice in as many days. It was a magnificent body.

"I missed you," he said.

"I missed you, too. I was hoping you would call."

"I'm here. Isn't that just as good?"

"It's better, Johnny. I—can I get you a drink? Are you hungry? I could scramble a few eggs or toss some sandwiches together or something."

"No, Jan."

"Then what can I give you?"

He answered her with a kiss. Again he thought he detected a trace of subtle resistance before she melted into the embrace. Her back muscles were slightly stiff, her body a bit distant, until her mouth opened and she relaxed against him, relaxed into passion. He wondered whether the stiffness, the detachment, had always been present. Probably, he decided. Probably he had failed to notice them before only because he had not been looking for them.

And because she was an actress.

"Oh," she said. "I see."

"Do you?"

"Uh-huh." She was a kitten now, a sexy kitten with deep smoky eyes and moist lips. It was a role that suited her.

"I see now," she went on. "Somebody came over because somebody wants to make love. I see it all now."

He kissed her neck. Her hands rubbed the back of his neck and played with his hair.

"You need a haircut, Johnny."

"I know."

"And that's not all you need, is it? You need more than a haircut. You need me."

He kissed her again. This time there was no tension at all—none he could detect, at any rate. This time there was passion and a low-burning flame.

Her voice was husky when she spoke. The husky purr of a sexy kitten.

"Come on, Johnny. You know where the bedroom is. Let's go there. Let's go from the living room to the loving room, Johnny. Let's go."

They walked to the bedroom and he closed the door. She turned to him, kissed him. Then she reached for the light switch. He took her hand.

"Leave it on, Jan."

"You want to watch?"

"I want to watch."

I want to watch your face, he thought. I want to see your eyes and your mouth when I feed you the right line. I want to see how good an actress you are, Jan.

She kissed him again. She stepped away, watched while he took off his jacket. He hung it on the knob of the closet door. Then she snuggled close to him and undid his tie.

"You just stand there," she told him. "I'm going to undress you. I can be a better servant than Ito, Johnny. Just stand there while I take your clothes off."

She took off the tie, then unbuttoned the shirt. "No bandages," she said. "Doctor take them off?"

"I took them off."

"Then I'd better not hug you," she said. "That's going to be rough. I like to hug you."

She finished removing his clothes, placed them neatly on the chair. He kicked off shoes and socks. She stepped back a stride or two and regarded him thoughtfully.

"Lovely," she said.

He gazed at her, his eyes properly passionate, as she unbelted her wrapper with casual grace, slipped it off and tossed it at the chair. She turned to face him, posed her ivory body for him, smiled at him.

"Do you like the merchandise, Mr. Lane?"

He moistened his lips with his tongue. He swallowed. He nodded.

All the proper gestures, he thought. All the right moves. All perfectly natural, all completely calculated to convey a certain erroneous, not to say erogenous, impression.

She came to him. He took her in his arms and felt her

nude body against his. Her breasts pressed against his chest and her mouth kissed his mouth. He found a breast with a hand and held it gently, tenderly.

"Let's go to bed," she murmured.

And they went to bed. Only it wasn't a bed at all, he realized. It looked like a bed, but it was something else entirely, something quite different.

It was a stage.

It began.

It went on.

It ended.

He held her for a moment afterward, held her warmth against him, and he wished that he did not have to do it, that he did not have to pile false tenderness on top of false passion. He felt like a prostitute and he felt like an actor—felt like almost anything save a decent human being.

Then he rolled away from her. The overhead light glared now. He heard the sound of a match striking. Then she was passing him a cigarette. He dragged on it and sucked the smoke into his lungs. He needed it.

Badly.

It had been weird, frightening. Love-making with all the trappings of love present and none of them meaning a thing. There was no desire on his part, no emotional attachment, nothing but the physical manifestation of excitement necessary for the accomplishment of his role.

He had gone through all the motions, all the kissing and

stroking and nuzzling and fondling. And then the scene had reached its climax, and so had they.

And it meant less than nothing.

"Johnny—"

The denouement, he thought. The beginning of the end. The conversation afterward.

"Johnny—"

"I needed that," he murmured.

"Me, too."

"You're good, Jan. You're wonderful."

"Am I?"

"Uh-huh."

"You're good, too."

He hesitated, but just for the merest shadow of a second. Then, his voice the same level, the same pitch, he read his line.

His eyes were on her face. He watched her eyes, watched her mouth, and he read his line perfectly.

He said: "As good as Elaine?"

The reaction was there. It was small and quick because she was a professional actress, but it was there because the line had taken her completely by surprise. She had been unprepared, totally unprepared. He saw her eyes widen instinctively, saw her mouth go weak. Her muscles tightened involuntarily.

"I don't get it," she said.

But she was lying. She got it, got it completely. He wished he had been wrong, but he had not been.

"I'll spell it out," he said. "You're a lesbian, Jan. Not a typical one. Not a swaggering type wearing pants and a tie. But then, neither was Elaine."

"You're out of your mind."

"Like hell I am. You met Elaine through the play. One of you made a pass at the other. God knows who threw the first pass. It hardly matters. It was what you both wanted, so you went to bed."

Jan was staring at him and he watched her eyes. Fury had joined the shock. But there was something else present, something that was a combination of fear and calculation. He could almost see the wheels turning within her brain.

"But Elaine had big ideas," he went on. "Maybe she got a look at your apartment and saw what a hole she was living in by comparison. Maybe she was planning a blackmail pitch from the first. She was a mercenary little minx, according to what I've heard from her East Side friends." Johnny butted his cigarette. "So she set it up," he went on. "With a tape recorder? Photographs? Whatever she got on you could hurt. All the rumors drifting in from California had helped rather than harmed. The Sex Goddess image was fine—letting the great American public think that little Jan Vernon had a streak of nymphomania under her soft skin, that kind of thing paid off at the box office. But the public wouldn't come running to watch a dyke play heterosexual love scenes . . ."

"You just made love to me," she gasped. "You just made love to me. How can you think anything like that?"

Johnny ignored the supplication in her voice.

"You would have paid, I suppose," he went on. "But Elaine got too ambitious. A friend of hers told me she was looking for big money. She had ideas about a penthouse apartment and a lush wardrobe. You couldn't afford that kind of double expense. Besides, your pride must have been hurt. Here you thought you had a lover and it turned out you had a blackmailer. You must have hated her one hell of a lot, Jan. I can't say I blame you."

Jan's eyes now were burning up with hate and the hatred was not for Elaine James. It was for Johnny.

"So you paid her off in spades, Jan. You went up to that rathole of hers and you took her to bed. First you made love to her and then you cut her throat. That was a nice macabre touch. I bet you got a kick out of it."

"You filthy son of a—"

"Shut up, will you? You left her dead and you came back here and went to work. You were in the clear for the time being but you couldn't be too sure of getting through a close police investigation. If Elaine James had been killed because she was Elaine James you were in trouble. You decided to make it look as though she had been killed because she was in *A Touch of Squalor.* You got on the phone and called people. You even called me, and I didn't recognize your voice. The whisper was cute, Jan. You wound up with a voice that could have belonged to a man or a woman. Everybody assumed it was a man. It was natural to do so."

He took a deep breath. He wished it were over, but there was more he had to get out.

"You told me about the calls you'd received." Johnny started to dress himself. "That was a pretty touch, too. Nobody else got a phone call before Elaine was killed. Only afterward—because you made them. But you let me think there really had been a caller before. You told me about the calls you got and about the calls Elaine got. And Elaine wasn't around to deny anything."

"You're crazy, Johnny. Absolutely mad."

"Sure I am. Or I would have seen through this a long time ago. You figured that the killing, of itself, might not be enough to prove that Elaine's death was a move against the show. So you lined up Rugger and Marlo to hand me a beating. I should have doped that out when I talked to Rugger. He told me the person on the phone whispered to him. I could understand the caller whispering to people in the cast—that meant they could recognize his voice otherwise. But you whispered to Rugger for a different reason. You whispered to him and Marlo to keep them from knowing you were a woman. You called them a second time while I was circling the block like an idiot. That was why you wanted me back after the cast meeting. You wanted to set me up for them."

"I wanted you to—to make love to me."

"Sure you did." He looked at her and wondered how she had missed grabbing up an Oscar during all those years in Hollywood. She was certainly a good enough actress. A peach of an actress—in bed or out of it. A star.

"So we went to bed," he said. "Then I left you and got my head kicked in by the talent you hired. You thought that beating, plus the murder, would set the stage to leave you in the clear—since it seemed indicated that the killer had it in for the whole show cast, rather than just Elaine."

"Then what about Tracy? Why would I do him in, too? You're being completely ridiculous, Johnny."

He stuck his legs into his trousers. "I found out that Elaine had someone on the hook for blackmail. Tracy fitted the part. I made the mistake of calling you and telling you about it. And that got you scared. You knew damn well that Tracy wasn't the blackmail victim, or the killer, either. And you cleverly figured out that once Tracy was cleared, the police would be out hunting for another blackmail victim. And the one they would turn up would be you." He sighed. "That took care of Tracy. You saw a way to kill two birds with one razor, to coin a phrase. With Tracy out of the way the blackmail angle would be dropped. And there would be a second murder on the string, a second member of the cast of *A Touch of Squalor* who was dead as a lox. It was a perfect deception play. Besides, you couldn't have liked Tracy too much. He was a seducer, a braggart, a pompous son of a bitch. The way you killed him was a pure poetic justice, come to think of it."

Her eyes tried to mock him. "Tell me all about it, Johnny. Tell me how I killed him. And why it was so poetic."

"Sure. You figured it would be a good idea to kill him the same way you killed Elaine. That would make it look like a chain murder, tie it up neater. You went to his apartment, got past the doorman as easily as you slipped by the one in my building that night. You took the elevator to the floor below and walked up a flight of stairs. He let you in and you fell into his arms and covered the poor bastard with kisses. Then you took him to bed."

Johnny paused to tie his shoes.

"But I don't suppose he got to make love to you—unless you wanted to be especially rotten about it. You probably cut his throat first. Why make love to a man if you can avoid it? Women were more your cup of tea. You killed him and left him there. You went home and let me find the body. And you were in the clear, or at least you thought you were." He forced a smile. "Interesting?"

"Fascinating. Tell me more, Johnny."

He shrugged. "About that night you tried to get me to drop the case," he said. "I wouldn't let go of it. So you came up to my building, to my apartment. You even picked the lock to get in. When I got home you were waiting for me. I should have learned enough from Rugger to figure that you were the killer. But I hadn't. I suppose that saved my life. You must have been all prepared to cut my throat if I seemed to know too much."

Having knotted his tie, he sat down on the bed, where she still was lying.

"That's fascinating," she told him. She stretched out her arms, one hand resting lightly on his thigh, the other draped over the side of the bed. The hand on his thigh began to do things. And he knew why. The last refuge of a woman, the ultimate appeal . . . He picked up the hand and moved it away. He did not want her to touch him, not now. It had been bad enough before when he was playing the role. Now it was too much to take.

"Let's get back to that razor," she went on. "If I remember correctly, I wasn't wearing too much when I saw you that night. I was nude, as I recall. Wasn't I?"

"Yeah."

"And you saw that my hands were empty. I couldn't have had the razor up a sleeve since I wasn't wearing any sleeves. Now if I had this razor, Johnny, where the hell was it?"

He shrugged. "Who knows?"

"It must have been somewhere," she said. "Unless I was just there because I wanted to make love to you. Unless this pipe dream of yours is a load of nonsense."

"Who the hell cares where it was?" he snapped. "You could have stuck it anywhere. You probably slipped it under the mattress."

Jan moved quickly. One moment she was lying flat on her back, one hand near his side, the other draped over the edge of the bed. The next second she was on her feet between the bed and the door.

"You were right," she said. "It was under the mattress. That's a good place for a razor, don't you think?"

He stared.

Because the razor wasn't under the mattress now.

It was in her hand.

Chapter Fifteen

Johnny Lane took a long look at the girl and a longer look at the razor. He also took a deep breath. And then he started to get up from the bed.

"Stay where you are, Johnny."

He did not stay. He stood up and looked at her. She was about ten feet from him—a couple of steps and he could reach her. But she had the razor.

"You'd do better not to kill me," he told her levelly. "Ito knows where I am. He knows everything I know. Besides, you'd be killing me in your bedroom instead of mine. That would be a little hard to explain."

She gave him a look of pure hatred. Fortunately, he thought, looks could not kill. But razors could.

"You might as well give up, Jan," he said, stalling.

Her laughter was shrill, chilling. "I should give up? I've got the razor, Johnny. Why should I give up?"

"Because you can't get away with killing me," he told her. "And on the other hand you can't get out of here unless you do kill me. You wouldn't get too far running stark naked through the streets. A girl draws a lot of attention that way. And I'm not only between you and your clothes—I'm between you and the closet." He knew he had to keep stalling—so he could think, so he could distract her from the razor. "Just for the hell of it," he said, "how right was I? Any mistakes?"

"Not many."

"Set me straight."

Her eyes narrowed. "You made it a little too coldblooded, Johnny. I wasn't planning on killing Elaine."

"No?"

"No. That night, I got there a little while after Carter left. We had been—lovers—for only about two weeks, Elaine and I."

He studied her. She seemed oddly embarrassed, but she went on talking.

"We made love, Johnny. Good love. And then we were lying in each other's arms and she—she told me I was going to have to pay. Four hundred dollars a week, no less. She had made a tape recording of the two of us in bed. She said I would pay, or she would send the recording around. Copies to the scandal magazines. A copy to you. A few copies to important people in Hollywood. She wanted twenty thousand dollars a year to keep that recording silent. That's a lot of money, Johnny."

"Couldn't you argue her down?"

Jan let out a burst of that chill laughter. "I didn't even try. Maybe she would have settled for less, at the moment. But blackmail goes on forever, Johnny. It doesn't stop. You know that, don't you?"

He nodded. "She would have bled you white. She would

always have had a copy of the tape lying around somewhere. And you would pay as long as you lived."

"That's right."

"So you killed her. You just happened to have along a razor . . ."

She sighed. "It was her razor, Johnny."

"What?"

"Elaine's razor. I got out of bed and went to the bathroom to wash up. I opened the medicine cabinet and this razor was on the bottom shelf. She used a straight razor on her legs, see? She told me once that it had been her father's and she hung on to it for sentimental reasons. I don't know if that's the truth, but a couple of times I had watched her strop the razor and shave her legs. I—I even took the strop later. I have it now."

"So you grabbed the razor—"

"Yes. I walked back to the bedroom, still naked, holding the razor behind my back. I sat down on the edge of the bed and looked at her. She started to tell me what she was going to do with all the money I would be paying her. She said she was a little worried about income taxes. She didn't want to pay them but she thought they would pick her up for tax evasion. She thought maybe she should report some of the money as gambling winnings. I listened to a few minutes of that. Oh, I didn't kill her because of the money, Johnny. That's hard to believe, isn't it?"

"Sort of," he said. He was calculating whether he could risk a step now.

"It's the truth, though. I had been—with me, it was love,

Johnny. Perverted, unnatural, but real. I loved Elaine. And then this girl that I loved—she wanted to blackmail me. She was throwing all that love right back in my face."

"So you killed her."

"Yes."

Any second now, he thought. Any second it would be time to rush her, time to take the blade away from her. She was weakening. It seemed to Johnny that her hand—the one holding the razor—was beginning to tremble a little . . .

He wondered who would win. He would have to go in low and fast, and he would have to get her when she was not ready. But all he had was his body. She had a razor and she had already killed two people with it.

"I washed the razor," she said. "I was going to leave it there. Then I thought that maybe they would think it was just a sex killing, an unknown burglar or somebody who just happened to sneak into her room and kill her. So I didn't want them to know it was her razor. I took it along, and the strop." She looked away, but only for an instant. "I didn't know I'd be using it again, Johnny. Not then."

There was a lamp on the bedside table. He could throw it at her, try to catch her off-balance. It might work. But she started to talk again, and he wanted to listen.

"At first," Jan said, "I couldn't think about anything except getting away. I took enough time to dress and try to wipe my fingerprints off everything I had touched. Then I left. I was still shaking when I got here."

She was shaking now. The lamp, he thought. The lamp, and a quick toss at her head, and go in low . . .

She took a step toward him. "I'm going to walk to you," she told him. "You're in a corner. You can't get away. I'm going to walk in on you and I'm going to kill you, Johnny Lane."

She said it as casually as if she were telling him the time of day. She took another step—she was no more than six feet away, now. The light from the ceiling glinted off the blade of the razor. It hypnotized him the way a snake hypnotizes a bird.

"So you'll kill me," he heard himself saying. "Then what will you do?"

"It won't matter to you. You'll be dead."

"What'll you do, Jan?"

"Run," she said. "Get dressed and get out and run like hell. Just run."

"They'll catch you, Jan."

"Maybe not."

"They'll catch you. And they'll kill you. One more murder isn't going to help any."

"Won't hurt me, either. They can only kill me once. I might as well hang for three sheep as for two."

"Is that why you killed Tracy?" One more stall, Johnny thought. He bunched his muscles.

She studied him. "I killed Tracy to throw them off the trail," she said. "You figured it out neatly enough. No, I didn't make love to him first, Johnny. He wanted me. God, how he wanted me! A pass a day, day in and day out. So I went up to his goddamned penthouse and offered him my fair white body. He was positively drooling. We took off our clothes and got into bed and I looked at that rotten, superior smile of his and I cut his damned throat and watched him die."

She took another step toward Johnny.

No time to get ready. Only time to act, only time to move swiftly and efficiently.

He fell away from her, reaching at the same time for the lamp. His fingers closed around the base of it and he heaved it as hard as he could, throwing straight for her face. He let himself fall backward, then hit the wall with one hand and pushed off from it, coming at her right behind the lamp.

The lamp staggered her. She almost lost her footing but she did not let go of the razor. He saw it coming at him in a downward arc as he pulled into her. Then he felt it bite into his side as the two of them sprawled to the floor. He had landed on top of her. He heard the air whoosh out of her lungs and he saw her jaw go slack. He got up. She got up.

The razor stayed on the floor.

She looked much younger without the razor. She looked younger and weaker and very unfortunate. His eyes scanned her naked body, her empty face. He tried to see her as an object of sexual desire, as something of love. Or as something to hate or fear.

He could see her only as a broken woman, to be pitied. He glanced from her to the blade on the floor. It was no longer a murder weapon. It was a toy, the latest addition to the prop inventory. It was silly to think that two persons had been killed with such a toy.

He looked at her again. Her mouth worked for a minute before any words came out.

"Just for the record, Johnny," she said quietly, "you're lousy in bed."

He had heard that one before. He thought back to Sondra, Sondra Barr with the violet eyes and the lovely red-gold hair.

"Real lousy," insisted Jan.

"That's because I'm not a girl," Johnny said.

His answer surprised her. And hers surprised him. "Aren't you going to hit me, Johnny?"

He shook his head. Was this what she expected of men? That in the last analysis they would beat her? No wonder she preferred girls.

"Then what are you going to do?"

"I'm going to take you to a cop named Haig," he announced, "and you're going to tell him just how you murdered two people."

Chapter Sixteen

She sat next to Johnny in the back seat of the taxi to Police Headquarters. The razor and the strop were in his pocket. He did not say a word during the ride. Neither did she.

He told the desk sergeant he was going in to see Haig. The cop started to give him directions.

"I know the way," Johnny told him. "I've been here often enough. And don't tell him I'm coming. It's a surprise."

It was a surprise. It was not a pleasant surprise, judging by the look on Haig's face. To be perfectly accurate, Johnny thought, you could only say that Haig turned purple. Literally. His face was the color of grape juice.

"That's right," Johnny insisted. "I've caught your killer for you."

"Once a night oughta be enough," the big cop said. "You wanta spend a week in jail, Johnny?"

He laughed. "This is Jan Vernon, Sam."

"We've met. Listen, Johnny—"

"Miss Vernon is a beautiful woman," he went on. "Also an accomplished actress."

"Dammit, Johnny—"

He glanced at Jan. "Also a murderess," he went on. "She

killed Elaine James and Carter Tracy. She tried to kill me but she failed, which explains my presence."

If Haig's face had not already turned purple, it would have then. He started to yell at Johnny, then changed his mind and turned to Jan.

"You want to press charges for criminal slander?" he said. "You got a witness. And this bastard's rich. You'd get a nice settlement out of the deal."

Johnny shook his head. "She won't sue me, Sam. She'll give you a confession instead. I've got the razor in my pocket, the one she used on both of them. You'd better get a stenographer in here for a statement. Jan feels talkative."

Haig started to say something. Then, evidently, he noticed the look in Jan Vernon's eyes for the first time.

So he did not say anything.

Nobody did, not for a second or two. Then Jan cleared her throat.

"He's telling the truth," Jan said. "You'd better get that steno. I'll tell you all about it."

"If you're looking for an apology," Haig said, "I've got news for you. You can go straight to hell."

Johnny looked out of the window. They were still in Haig's office, and night had given away to dawn. Jan's statement had been dictated, typed and signed. Jan had been led off and locked up. Soon, Johnny thought, he would go home. And sleep for thirty-six hours. At the very least.

"So you came up with the killer," Haig chided. "But you

did it back-asswards, Johnny boy. You should have come straight to me, Johnny. What would you have lost that way?"

"A case," Johnny said.

"Huh?"

"The evidence against that girl wasn't enough to stuff a thimble with it. Nothing could have been proved until she cracked."

"We would have broken her."

"Sure—if you hammered away long enough. But be reasonable, Sam. What would you have done if I had come in here tonight—last night, whenever the hell it was. What would you have done if I had handed it to you? No evidence, no proof. Just an idea."

"We would have picked her up."

"Be honest for a minute, Sam. Drop the *Dragnet* routine. You would have thrown me out on my ear."

"Well, after the bit with Buell . . ."

"That's what I mean. Even if you went through the motions, you never would have dragged it out of her. I managed to. So why yell at me? I handed you a killer, didn't I?"

Haig looked at his desk. Then the desk grew boring, and he turned to look through the window. That was no better. Finally he looked at Johnny.

"If I produced a play," he said carefully, "and—"

"That'll be the day."

"Listen to me," Haig said. "Hear me out. Let's say I produce a play. Let's say the critics like it. Let's say the audience likes it. Let's say it runs for three years and the movies buy it for a quarter of a million dollars."

"All right—let's say it."

"Let's," Haig agreed. "Now wouldn't you be madder than hell?"

It was seven in the morning when Johnny got home. Ito, of course, was still awake. Or had just awakened. No matter what time it was, you could always be certain of two things. The sun had not yet set on the British Empire, and Ito was awake.

"Jan did it," Johnny said. "Someday I'll explain the whole thing. But not now."

Ito nodded.

Johnny said pleasantly, "I am going to sleep. No calls, no telegrams, no anything. I am going to sleep. I shall slumber for thirty-six hours. Maybe longer."

He was wrong, of course. No human being sleeps for thirty-six hours, unless he had just finished fighting a losing battle with a tsetse fly. It is impossible to sleep for thirty-six hours, and Johnny didn't.

He woke up after twenty-nine.

At which point he tried to fall asleep again. And failed.

Ito wisely said nothing until after breakfast and coffee and the first cigarette of the morning.

"There were quite a few phone calls," he said then. "The news-papers, mostly."

"What did you tell them?"

"To go to hell in a handbasket," quoted Ito inscrutably. "Was that the right thing to say?"

"Better to go to hell," remarked Johnny, "on wheels. Any other calls?"

"One from Ernest Buell. He wants you to call him. He says that, although you are a son of a female dog, so is everyone else in show business, including himself. He still wants to direct *A Touch of Squalor* if and when you manage to reassemble a cast. He realizes that it will not be easy to replace a murderess and her two victims, but that he'd love to help, and you should call him."

"I will." Johnny said. "Any others?"

"The author of *A Touch of Squalor.* He wants to know what's going to happen to his play."

"He's not the only one. Anybody else?"

Ito thought for a moment. "One more," he said. "That young bearded Zen. The hand-clapper."

"Lennie? Yeah, I thought he'd call. He wants me to give him a job. I'll have to find something for him to do."

"He doesn't want a job."

"You sure?"

Ito nodded positively. "Matter of fact, he wanted to make an appointment with you. A business appointment."

"Of course. You see, I told him I'd get him some sort of job in the theater. The production end of things. Something to do so he can learn the business—"

But Ito was shaking his head. "He said to tell you that he read the story in the newspapers. He said that the theater seems a little too risky. 'A cat only lives once, he might as well live as long as he can.' I think those were the words he used."

"Then," Johnny asked, puzzled, "what in hell does he want from me?"

"He said he wants to sell you some life insurance," Ito explained. "He said nobody else would do you such a favor. Because, he said, you're a terrible risk."

A new afterword by the author

I don't seem to remember writing *Strange Embrace*.

Oh, I know it's mine. I can tell by flipping through it that I did indeed write it, and in fact I remember having written it. But I have no recollection of being at work on the book, or where I was when I wrote it. I'm pretty sure I know what I was paid for writing it—$1000, as I recall, which would come to $900 for me and $100 for Scott Meredith, who was representing me at the time. I know there were never any royalties (or if they were, they were all for Scott Meredith). I've learned through the miracle of Google Books that an Australian edition was published, with the title changed to *Act One: Murder!* and Ben Christopher's name on the cover, and that never brought me a dime, or the Aussie equivalent thereof.

I'm not complaining, mind you. Just letting you know what I remember, and what I don't.

Strange Embrace started life as an assignment, which came to me from Beacon Books via Scott Meredith. What they wanted was a mystery novel of 50,000 words or so based on a TV series called *Johnny Midnight*. Edmund O'Brien played Johnny, a theatrical producer with a wise-cracking Japanese houseboy. The series ran for 39 episodes in 1959–60, which is to say it ran for a year. Back then you ran new stories for nine months and then gave way to a summer replacement. Nowadays a full season is what, 26 episodes? 22?

Well, it turns out that 39 episodes of *Johnny Midnight* was more than enough. Edmund O'Brien's girth may have had something to do with this. He'd put on a substantial amount of weight since he starred in the noir film classic, *D.O.A.*, and the producers of the TV show tried to save things by putting the poor sonofabitch on a crash vegetarian diet. He may have lost a pound or two, but he didn't pick up many viewers, and the network waved bye-bye after a single season.

Now this was not the first TV show shot out from under me. That distinction belongs to *Markham,* which starred Ray Milland, and which also quit the airways after a single season. And, *mirabile dictu*, both of these TV wonders emanated from the same studio. (Revue, back then, later Universal Studios.)

What exactly did they want me to do?

Beacon Books wanted me to write a tie-in novel. I'd be making use of the characters from the TV series and fashioning an original plot for them. There were a lot of TV tie-in novels back then, and I guess they sold well enough, if the shows on which they were based were themselves popular. If not, not; if nobody would watch the show for free, why would anyone shell out 35¢ to read a printed version thereof?

So that was the assignment, and I said okay. Why not? I'd already done this sort of thing once by then.

*   *   *

In fact I'd done it twice. It was Belmont Books that commissioned *Markham,* and I sat down and wrote it, and it turned out rather well. At least I thought so, and I showed it to Don Westlake, and he thought so, too, and Henry Morrison (who represented me at Scott Meredith) read it and agreed with both of us, and sent it over to Knox Burger at Gold Medal, who bought it and paid me $2500 for it. I changed Roy Markham's name to Ed London and called the book *Coward's Kiss,* and Gold Medal changed the title to *Death Pulls a Doublecross*, and it came out in due course as the second book published under my own name. (It's since been republished a few times, and it's *Coward's Kiss* once again. If you can just outlast the bastards, sooner or later you get to set things right.)

Then I had to fulfill my obligation to Belmont, and I wrote a book I called *Markham,* and they kept the title and added a subtitle: *The Case of the Pornographic Photos.* Isn't that catchy? It sounds like Nancy Drew gone wrong. It's now available as an Open Road ebook with the title I gave it when a paperback publisher reprinted it some years ago: *You Could Call It Murder.* It has my name on it, but then it always did.

Strange Embrace.

I was living in New York when I wrote it, but whether it was just before or just after we moved from 110 West 69th Street to 444 Central Park West I couldn't tell you.

I do know this much: By the time I delivered the book, which wouldn't have been more than three weeks after I started work on it, *Johnny Midnight* was history. The same fate fell upon *Markham*, but Belmont went ahead and published it all the same, fulfilling their agreement with Revue, and perhaps figuring that the Ray Milland connection wouldn't hurt the book's chances, even if the series was toast. Maybe there was no way to get out of their contract with Revue. Who knows? The series was dead, but the book went to the printer all the same.

It was a different story at Beacon. They had to buy the book, they were fine with the book, but why pay money to a TV studio to tie in with a piece-of-shit series that nobody watched in the first place? So one of their editors went to work, changing Johnny's last name from Midnight to Lane. (Hey, why not? It could have been worse. "There but for the grace of God goes Johnny Daybreak.")

They hung their own title on it. I'd called it *Johnny Midnight,* imaginatively enough, and they picked *Strange Embrace,* which gave me a titular hat trick—three novels under three different names, each with the word *strange* in it. (*Strange Are the Ways of Love*, by Lesley Evans; *A Strange Kind of Love*, by Sheldon Lord; and, duh, *Strange Embrace*, by Ben Christopher.) Each title was the publisher's contribution. Nobody asked me.

Neat, huh? I'd have to call it weird. Even eerie. Or— what's the word I'm looking for?

Oh, right. *Strange.*

*   *   *

About the pen name.

Why did I use one? If my first tie-in novel, *Markham,* was respectable enough to have my own name on it, why slap a pen name on *Johnny Midnight?*

I don't remember what I was thinking at the time, but my guess is that it had something to do with the publisher. Beacon was a pretty cheesy house, a second-rate publisher of soft-core erotica, and who would put his own name on a Beacon book? (Well, Charles Willeford would and did, but then it's hard to find a rule to which Charles wasn't an exception. Fine man, brilliant writer, and *sui generis* as all get out.)

But why Ben Christopher?

Right around this time, my great good friend Don Westlake also wrote a TV tie-in, and used the name Ben Christopher on it. It was, he said, his name for tie-ins. Well, how would it be if I used it for one of mine? He said it would be fine, because he figured he was done with it, and done with tie-ins.

So just now I tried to find out what tie-in novel Don did, and it turned out he didn't—not a book, that is. He seems to have used the name one time only, on a story that appeared in *77 Sunset Strip Magazine.* It was very likely the lead story, unquestionably a tie-in, and probably novella length. But it wasn't a book. I seem to be the only person to have used the name Ben Christopher on a book.

Strange, innit?

Lawrence Block
Greenwich Village

My Newsletter: I get out an email newsletter at unpredictable intervals, but rarely more often than every other week. I'll be happy to add you to the distribution list. A blank email to lawbloc@gmail.com with "newsletter" in the subject line will get you on the list, and a click of the "Unsubscribe" link will get you off it, should you ultimately decide you're happier without it.

About the Author

Lawrence Block has been writing award-winning mystery and suspense fiction for half a century. His newest book, a sequel to his greatly successful Hopper anthology *In Sunlight or in Shadow*, is *Alive in Shape and Color*, a 17-story anthology with each story illustrated by a great painting; authors include Lee Child, Joyce Carol Oates, Michael Connelly, Joe Lansdale, Jeffery Deaver and David Morrell. His most recent novel, pitched by his Hollywood agent as "James M. Cain on Viagra," is *The Girl with the Deep Blue Eyes*. Other recent works of fiction include *The Burglar Who Counted The Spoons*, featuring Bernie Rhodenbarr; *Keller's Fedora*, featuring philatelist and assassin Keller; and *A Drop Of The Hard Stuff*, featuring Matthew Scudder, brilliantly embodied by Liam Neeson in the 2014 film, *A Walk Among The Tombstones*. Several of his other books have also been filmed, although not terribly well. He's well known for his books for writers, including the classic *Telling Lies For Fun & Profit* and *Write For Your Life*, and has recently published a collection of his writings about the mystery genre and its practitioners, *The Crime Of Our Lives*. In addition to prose works, he has written episodic television (*Tilt!*) and the Wong Kar-wai film, *My Blueberry Nights*. He is a modest and humble fellow, although you would never guess as much from this biographical note.

Email: lawbloc@gmail.com
Twitter:@LawrenceBlock
Facebook: lawrence.block
Website: lawrenceblock.com